THE GEORGES'

Elizabeth Jolley was born in the industrial Midlands of England in 1923. She moved to Western Australia in 1959 with her husband and three children. She has worked in a variety of occupations and is currently cultivating a small orchard and teaching part-time at Curtin University of Technology.

Elizabeth Jolley is acclaimed as one of Australia's leading writers and has received an AO, an honorary doctorate (Hon. D. Tech.) from WAIT, now Curtin University, and the ASAL Gold Medal for her contribution to Australian literature. Australian literary journals and anthologies have published her fiction and poetry which, together with her plays, have been broadcast on British and Australian radio. She has published three collections of short fiction, a collection of short essays, *Central Mischief*, and ten novels, of which *Mr Scobie's Riddle* and *My Father's Moon* won the *Age* Book of the Year Award, *Milk and Honey* the New South Wales Premier's Award, *The Well* the Miles Franklin Award, and *Cabin Fever*, the FAW ANA Literature Award.

In 1993, *The Sugar Mother* won the France-Australia Literary Translation Award, *Central Mischief* won the Historical and Critical Studies Prize and the Premier's Prize at the Western Australian Premier's Book Awards, and *The Georges' Wife* was the *Age* Book of the Year.

Also by Elizabeth Jolley

THE GEORGES' WIFE

Elizabeth Jolley

Penguin Books

Penguin Books Australia Ltd
487 Maroondah Highway, PO Box 257
Ringwood, Victoria, 3134, Australia
Penguin Books Ltd
Harmondsworth, Middlesex, England
Viking Penguin, A Division of Penguin Books USA Inc.
375 Hudson Street, New York, New York 10014, USA
Penguin Books Canada Limited
10 Alcorn Avenue, Toronto, Ontario, Canada, M4V 3B2
Penguin Books (N.Z.) Ltd
182-190 Wairau Road, Auckland 10, New Zealand

First published in Viking by Penguin Books Australia, 1993
Published in Penguin, 1994
10 9 8 7 6 5 4 3 2 1
Copyright © Elizabeth Jolley, 1993

The author wishes to acknowledge the use of D.H. Lawrence's poem,
'Gloire de Dijon'.

Typeset in 11¼/12½ Sabon by Midland Typesetters Pty. Ltd.
Maryborough, Victoria.
Made and printed in Australia by Australian Print Group,
Maryborough, Victoria

National Library of Australia
Cataloguing-in-Publication data:

Jolley, Elizabeth, 1923–
The Georges' wife.

ISBN 0 14 023255 9

I. Title.

A823.3

For Leonard Jolley

ACKNOWLEDGEMENTS

I would like to express my thanks to the Curtin University of Technology for the continuing privilege of being with students and colleagues in the School of Communication and Cultural Studies and for the provision of a room in which to write. I would like, in particular, to thank Don Watts, Peter Reeves, Brian Dibble, Ian Reid, Anne Brewster and Don Grant. In addition I would like to thank John Maloney, John de Laeter, Don Yeats and Ross Bennett.

A special thanks is offered to Nancy McKenzie who, for a great many years, has typed my manuscripts. She is endlessly patient.

I would like as well to thank Kay Ronai, an especially thoughtful and sensitive editor.

'*Die mit Tränen säen, werden mit Freuden ernten*'
(They that sow in tears shall reap in joy)

'The smallest service done to the lowliest possesses an
eternal value.'

Evelyn Pearce

> *. . . when thy mind*
> *Shall be a mansion for all lovely forms,*
> *Thy memory be as a dwelling place*
> *For all sweet sounds and harmonies;*

Wordsworth

'Tell me about yourself, Migrant', the rice-farm widow says to me. So I tell my widow things about myself. When I tell her about Felicity and Noël her mouth is so wide open, as she listens, I can see her gold fillings. At that time, I think her whole fortune is in her mouth.

'You mean to tell me!' she says. 'Oh, I can't believe . . .' she says, 'that they, I mean, *together*. You can't mean *that*.'

'Yes, that's right,' I tell her.

'Oh, Migrant. You poor child, poor poor child.'

'Oh no, your widowship, not at all. Nothing like that. They were very gentle and considerate. They were intellectuals, don't you see. The whole thing was more of an *idea*. And it was quite a joke thing between us, between the three of us, every time. Their very good manners, don't you know.'

'More than once! Heavens, child!'

'Please, please – don't be concerned. Do not concern your gracious self; it was funny, really funny. They were, *unlike us*, so very polite.'

'You mean, "*after you*" and "Oh no, *after you*".'

'Well sort of, not quite, but yes, rather like that.'

'What an *experience* you had.'

'I suppose so.'

'You *suppose* so. My dear Migrant, do you realise that plenty of people would give their eye teeth . . .'

'But what would anyone *do* with someone else's eye teeth?'

THE ROADS

What are you thinking, I want to ask Mr George. What are you thinking about, I want to ask him. Are you thinking about Miss Eleanor and whether she will be coming home soon, I want to ask him.

From Harold Avenue we turn left into Hammond and left into Goldsworthy, cross Goldsworthy into Bernard and go on westward downhill, smooth smooth, to the park. My heels, the heels of my shoes, newly repaired, sound on the new surface of the road, like a trotting horse, a little trotting horse. Like a toy horse, Mr George makes this observation saying, at the same time, that his feet are not making any noise on the road.

From the park it is uphill into Thompson and then a right turn into Koeppe across Princess into Caxton, then Warwick and back along Queen. Queen Street is lined on both sides with old twisted trees. The long-leaved peppermints, they make a tunnel of shade and fragrance. In Queen it is like being in a green church or a small green cathedral. Does Mr George think so too, I want to ask him. Would he agree about a cathedral? Is a little street in a suburb, I want to ask him, a place of worship and of prayer?

There is hardly ever anyone about in the streets in the quiet afternoons. Sometimes the days, depending on the time of the year, are either too wet or too hot, but we are there, all the same.

Sometimes I think of asking Mr George does he remember when the girls were little and doing their spelling and arithmetic with Miss Eleanor. Does he remember now their piano practice, I want to ask. Does he remember the night porter with his springing hoop of keys at the hospital and does he, I want to ask, think of the farm, the derelict farm in the field by the coal mine. Does he, I almost ask, does he remember Dr Metcalf and his wife, Magda, and does he remember Noël and Felicity. Gertrude too, does he remember Gertrude? How can Mr George remember Gertrude except what he will have been told? It is likely he does not remember what I told him about her.

Do you remember the illness I had, I want to ask Mr George. Does Mr George remember my mother's reproachings over both the illness and the pregnancy, saying how is it that *as a doctor* I have been unable to avoid the particular illness, and *as a nurse* before that, stupid completely stupid about the pregnancy – just like a rabbit, breeding straight away, she said then, adding that she should never have given me the book about Elisabeth Ney, the sculptor because she, E. Ney, has a baby in that book without being married.

I remember my mother's repeated warnings about the illness. Mr George would not remember them. They were not directed at him.

When I ask Mr George if he remembers our long journey across the world, he says he is sorry he is such a silly old man and will I remind him. And when I ask him what he has had for lunch he does not know. And when I ask him what he does remember or if he asks a question himself, both his reply and his question are surprising to the point of being startling.

THE HOUR
OF THE WOLF

I often wish for a mountain or even two. I have the feeling that a sky line with hills and mountains would put the landscape into some sort of proportion. I think, quite often, that a well-proportioned landscape could help me to have a more balanced view of my life. I suppose the same could be said about seeing the well-balanced and pleasing proportions of a man or a woman, a perfect stranger, in the street or in a shopping centre.

Occasionally a warm fragrance in the days approaching summer prompts me to suggest to someone who is coming to my rooms to keep an appointment, that they take the path through the pines from the station. It is both a short cut and a pleasant little walk. A remedy.

The strange thing about living, I often nearly speak of this during a consultation, is the repetition. It is as though the individual enters the same experience again and again. The same kinds of people make the same demands, and the giver, blessed with giving, gives yet again in what turns out to be the wrong direction.

I am a shabby person. I understand, if I look back, that I have treated kind people with an unforgivable shabbiness. For my work a ruthless self-examination is needed. Without understanding something of myself, how can I understand anyone else.

Every day I am seeing people living from day to day, from one precarious day to the next, from one despairing week to the next, without any vision of any kind of future. I understand that I, at various times in my own life, have been unable to see anything beyond the immediate.

Every day the waiting room, outside my consulting room, is lined with people waiting. During the years I have become acquainted with all kinds of waiting rooms but have never waited in mine. I intend one day to be there early, earlier than the first appointment, to try out my waiting room as if it would be possible to be then shown in to my own consulting room . . .

Mr George is not straight in his frame. There is a white space at the bottom of the picture. When I take the back off the little silver frame of Mr George's photograph – just a head and shoulders with both ears showing as for a passport – I find a lock of his hair before it turned white. I don't see the hair at first but find it on the quilt and I can't, for a minute, think where it has come from. I hold it in my hand and then I understand Miss George must have put it there. It is a soft fair curl, perhaps from his first baby hair-cut.

Mr George during the time I have known him has always had white hair.

If I miss Mr George, it is something from before which I am missing. That is what he would say. But just now the glowing colours of the bricks in the path reflect in the soft breast feathers of the doves. It is likely that during the next consultation I shall heal myself. I shall try to put into ordinary words the verses from 1 Corinthians chapter 16 v.13 and 14

> *Watch ye, stand fast, in the faith,*
> *quit you like men, be strong*
> *let all your things be done with charity.*

'Be kind', my father always said. With kindness in mind, perhaps I shall suggest a little dwelling in thought on the reflection of warm brick colours and on the tender breasts of doves.

Sometimes I wonder whether, between the soft fair curl of baby hair and the white hair of an elderly man, Mr George had brown hair. This is the kind of thing it would not do to ask Miss George. If she had wanted me to know she would have told me.

What are you brooding on, Vera, in your silence, what are you brooding on?

I suppose I shall be lonely, Mr George, I suppose that, one day, I shall have to be alone. I shall be lonely.

I shall be lonely and alone without Mr George, Oliver really, but I always think of him as Mr George and that is the name I have for him. This way a continuity is not broken. Similarly Dr Metcalf was always Dr Metcalf. Silly, but that's how it was. In any case we do not talk now of Dr Metcalf.

Everything changes. Slowly everything changes. I am tired. Because of being tired I am irritable. Mr George can hear that I am impatient and it is as if he is crying somewhere quietly inside because of the tone in my voice. An old man, like a baby, is able to hear and to know the tone and he cries. If you go on being impatient and unkind, the feeling of remorse which follows is so powerful and terrible and there is no way of explaining that you are sorry. Remorse is irreversible and unforgettable and there is no way out from the pain of feeling it. There is nothing for me to do but to take Mr George's hands in my hands and stroke them and kiss them in an attempt to say I will not be impatient again. And then to try, for ever, to prevent anything which will bring it back – this remorse.

In every old man I suppose there are glimpses of his childhood which he will have forgotten and which did not show earlier. They would have been hidden in the conventional mannerisms and *face* necessary for household, for work and for community. These tiny transient appearances of certain behaviour, of wish and choice, of dignity and affection which I can see, from time to time, in Mr George reflect the shape, the pattern, the whim and the fancy in the ideas on upbringing held by Miss George.

There are too some things which seem to frighten him, or threaten, perhaps reminding vaguely of small punishments of some kind. Small things like spilling a glass of milk or scattering crumbs or not finishing a sandwich . . .

'How can Faust go on after what has happened?' a student asked Mr George during one of his lectures. Mr George explained then that Goethe gave Faust forgetfulness. 'Perhaps,' Mr George said, 'perhaps forgetfulness is the kindest blessing. But whether Goethe meant this is another matter.'

I sometimes went to Mr George's lectures simply to be where he was, to be in the same room, *in an ordinary sort of way*, where he was. Naturally it was with Miss George's approval that I went.

This might be as good a place as any to mention that it is perhaps a curious irony that my mother visiting the Georges did not come as a reader of Goethe, *Faust* or *Iphigenia*, for example, in Goethe's own language and having, in addition, the ability to discuss with Mr George his own favourite aspect that all guilt, in Goethe's interpretation, both human and that of the gods is avenged on earth. She came, not as someone who could, from her own reading and interest, offer detail from Goethe's own life – an example being, that as a young man he had insisted on his mother spreading out, for his choosing, three sets of clothing every morning – but she came as my mother, the mother of the maid and grandmother of the maid's two illegitimate babies and who had, as her best friend, the railway-man's widow, Mrs Pugh, living in the small house next door to her own small house.

My mother could have quoted Kestner's response to *Werther*, *il est dangereux d'avoir un auteur pour ami*, but in the presence of the Georges she did not seem to be that sort of person. So much do people alter themselves and equally do not recognise their own merit in the eyes of other people.

The Georges, I know now but did not understand then, would have welcomed this other aspect of my mother had she chosen – felt able, I should say, to offer it.

Perhaps it is true to say that both my mother and I, usually from necessity, have been able to present more than one face during both favourable and unfavourable times. I think that this is probably an acquired skill developed from a hidden gift at birth, which for some may never be needed.

Once I told Mr George that I was afraid he would leave me or that he would not want me any more and he, nursing me on his arm, told me that most people ultimately have the experience of having only the memory of love; except, of course, those who have never known what it is like to be in love, to love and to be loved. And even then, he said, most people will have some remembered cherishing or remembered feelings of cherishing towards someone else.

'I shall always love you and want you,' he told me then, 'but in the end we all do have to leave each other. Even when I do leave you,' he said, 'I shall have given you myself and you will be different because of knowing me. This is inescapable and it goes both ways.'

When I think of this it is necessarily true of Dr Metcalf and, in this idea of being different because of receiving certain intangible gifts, it is true too of my father and my mother, of Gertrude, of staff nurse Ramsden (even if mostly in my imagination), and of Miss George and even of my father's sister, my Aunt Daisy, or Miss Daisy as her housekeeper companion, Miss Clayton, called her.

One afternoon I wait for Mr George. I want to wait for Mr George and walk home with him from the university, feeling the palm of his hand pressed against my palm and our steps measuring, side by side, together on the pavement, and feeling the damp air of autumn fresh on my face and in my hair but mostly feeling his hand holding my hand and both of us, in this way, making the declaration of belonging to each other. So I wait for him.

As I begin to write now a feeling of peacefulness comes over me as if I need not for inexplicable half-ridden reasons refrain from writing any longer. Three things emerge; one is that a mother always forgives. The second is that it is often not possible to write about events until they are over or sufficiently of the past, that they can be regarded as being in that twilight between the fact and the imagined. There are tremulous and fragile boundaries; thin invisible lines of hoped-for coherence through which the writer moves with caution aware, all the time, of an emerging nakedness for which conventional clothes are too transparent. And thirdly; secrets, if they are revealed completely, become mere facts. Secrets, if partly kept, can be seen as relating not to some kind of imitation but to something extra to real life.

On that afternoon I do slip out of the house secretly to wait for Mr George on the corner where the trams stop and there is almost always a drunk, in an old coat, slumped over one of the smooth metal stumps which are along the edge of the pavement to stop people from rushing across the road in front of a tram.

I wait there in the cold darkening afternoon wishing to see him, fresh faced and smiling, his heavy overcoat unbuttoned and his scarf loose, coming down University Avenue. I think that it will be dark enough for us to walk without being noticed.

After waiting for what seems a terrible long time I telephone the house to see if he has gone home some other way. It seems silly and insolent of me to do this. Miss George answers, her kind elderly voice saying, 'Hello' and then the number. I hang up on her three times before going back there alone.

8

I suppose waiting for someone I really want to see at different times during the years reminds me all over again of that time, a long time ago, when I am cold and pregnant and not at all sure how things will turn out for me. That day I remember clearly, in the evening, Mr George telling Miss George about a student of his who laughs like the opening of the Bach cantata, the one with the exultant trumpet matching exquisitely with the superb voice of a boy soprano. Number fifty-two he thinks it is, 'Praise the Lord Everywhere Throughout the Land', perhaps not exactly those words but that is the meaning in the triumphant music.

When I tell Mr George later that I am jealous of the student and what was her name, he says he can't remember anything about her except her laugh.

'You must not be jealous,' he tells me then. 'You must always tell me how you feel,' he says then privately in the aprons hanging on the back of the kitchen door, one of his favourite hiding places for catching me quickly as I am going through. 'I must know everything about you,' he says, 'and I want you to be happy.'

To look at the back of someone's neck is to see how vulnerable the person is. The back of Mr George's neck is the same as it was when I first knew him. For Miss George that hidden and gentle place will have been hers to know at a much earlier time. The elder sister bringing up the younger brother, as she has done, her knowledge and her feelings might well be much greater than mine. I do not speak of this to Mr George.

Bay Road, Hammond, Harold and Goldsworthy, Bernard Street, the park, Thompson Road, Koeppe Road, Princess, Caxton, Warwick and Queen. Of these closely watched roads Goldsworthy is smooth and Hammond, because of the rough blue-chip metal, is uneven. Queen is fragrant and shaded with peppermint trees whereas Hammond has cape lilacs and plane trees which arch, dappled, overhead creating either a shelter from the sun when it is too hot, or from the rain when it comes. The delicate china blue of the washed sky, beyond the middle distance, created by the high, thin branches of the lilacs, is serene and impersonal. The leaves, turning, rustle and fall. They sound like approaching footsteps and then they collect in softly whispering drifts.

Some days Mr George, not remembering, feels he is lost.

Watch the hedges I tell him, look closely at the honeysuckle, the hibiscus, the oleander, the rosemary and the raging plumbago. Look, I tell him, at the roses, the white roses and the red. Look at the bougainvillaea, the purple, the pink and the apricot and, over there, the wistaria. You are not lost I tell him, I am with you.

Our walk is smooth smooth purring along Goldsworthy and smooth smooth down Bernard, westward to the park. Because of the new blue-chip metal Hammond is rough. From the back I can see closely the back of Mr George's neck. The back of the neck, the nape, is vulnerable. From behind the wheelchair there is the close view of the back of the neck of the person who is sitting in the chair.

Sometimes I wake too early at that time described as the hour of the wolf. I think then of all the books and papers, the pictures and the cassettes, the dishes, the linen and the clothes and the furniture in the house. I think of the shabby paint and the deep cracks in the walls and the ceilings. And then there are the places where the roof leaks. I go round in the dark, putting pails and bowls to catch the dripping rain water. This house has, between the corrugated-iron gables, a flat roof similar to the flat roof years ago where I shovelled off the snow, when I was young and not at all fearful of the height of the ladder, perched on the top landing, with all the flights of stairs curving down, below me, down to the front hall. A flat roof, we all agreed at that time, gives the most trouble.

A flat roof is the worst kind of roof – Miss George always made the announcement on wet mornings in that other house.

She was sure the wind had brought all the soaked leaves from the surrounding streets into the space between the gables.

Suffering is like art we create it within ourselves. Noël said this and said it was written by Strindberg. Felicity, as usual, answered Noël with a second quotation; 'Look,' she said, '*at the ruin of the individual when he isolates himself . . .*' 'Strindberg again,' Noël said.

It does not seem possible to avoid either of these truths. I am confronted daily in my consulting rooms with manifestations of both.

The raw inhospitable remains of the night are captured by the surprise of the morning. This soft patience waits outside the closed blinds where birds, unconcerned, squabble endlessly, perhaps going over the roosting disagreements of the previous evening.

Perhaps it can be said that the only thing in favour of blinds is the revelation when they are released in the mornings. This revelation is always forgotten during that hour when life is at its lowest ebb, that hour years ago when I was nursing; and in the stillness perhaps between three and four in the morning, a life, hovering, would slip away for ever and Sister Bean, for thirty years the Night Superintendent, would add to her bedside prayers, while still on her knees, a reprimand saying that nurses should remember that they were only nurses and should not think of themselves as being capable of controlling the Divine Intervention.

This revelation, when the blinds are released in the mornings, is in the daylight which is so steadily and reassuringly increasing as if suggesting that, with the rising of the sun every morning, everything will be as usual. And that all I have to do is to go out into the new day in an ordinary way, as usual.

Every morning with the orange juice, that is when I am squeezing the small oranges for juice, I put aside a glassful for Mr George. A libation, you could call it that. And I drink my own share straight off and look up at the sky.

Every morning I understand that this is the only time when

I remember to look, with suitable undisturbed humbleness, at the sky. As a well-proportioned and balanced landscape can help towards a balanced view of all that belongs to living, the high up, often clear limitless space of the early morning sky can be a reminder of my own insignificance. Feeling insignificant like this helps to bring about a measured sense of proportion.

This morning, during my homage to the sky, I see something I have not thought about for years. I see in the slow-moving, white masses of cloud, without any previous remembering or thought, the face of a ram. The ram which was caught by his horn on a branch of a small gnarled fruit tree in an orchard beyond the top field at Gertrude's Place. I was there with Gertrude very early as I had gone on my day off from the hospital to fetch black-market eggs for my mother. At that time, during the war, I was nursing and I went to Gertrude's Place, on my bicycle, whenever I could. As always the clouds seemed low, as they often do in the country, over the field. I felt that I could reach up and touch them with both hands. The sky there was often like this, especially when it was about to rain. We were walking round the field she wanted me to have and we pushed through the hedge into the orchard which belonged to someone else but which, Gertrude maintained, we could buy if I came in with her on the idea she had about me owning the field and the two of us having a pig there and a sty built. A few sheep, unconcerned, moved in gently closing circles together between the neglected trees. We came upon the ram by accident. Gertrude said that he must have been there, hooked on the low branch, for some time. She said she thought the tree was an apple tree. She said to look at the way the bark had been rubbed smooth with the ram trying to free himself.

The dignified gentle expression in the cloud ram's face matches, in my memory, the dignified patience in the eyes of the exhausted and starved ram imprisoned on the low twisted branch.

On that day, Gertrude showed me how to push and pull the ram to get him free. 'His horns, the shape of 'em,' she said, 'are against him.' She explained that an animal was not the same as a human. Lacking human imagination the ram would not have been thinking and anticipating the suffering of being trapped and slowly starving to death as a human being would. The ram, she said, would pause in his struggles and then resume them and a bit later on would pause once more and so on. But he would not *think*, she said, in between times, that he was trapped.

When, at last, we managed to free the ram he tottered and fell over and Gertrude said that, if I did not mind, we must have him up on his legs. So we tried once more and he started off after the sheep in a crazy sort of way. Gertrude said then that he would fall again and not be able to get up and he would die. He had that look about him, she said, but since he wasn't her ram there was not much use in us hanging about there.

We wrapped the eggs in threes, in sheets of newspaper and in pages torn from magazines. I wanted to tell Gertrude about a forthcoming party at the Metcalfs' but already, by this time, she was for urging me to let those people alone and had, more than once, offered to visit them to ask them not to invite me to their house and their ways. Gertrude had two dressed fowls as well for my mother, as usual. And, as usual, she explained that one of them had had a fox get to her but not all that much taken, just a wing and a bit of breast. She had neatened the damage, she said, with her dress-making scissors. 'Tell Mother,' she said, 'I'm sorry about that old red fox.'

It seems strange now to remember small things from years ago. Perhaps remembering them means that they are not so small.

Remembering the dignified gentleness in the eyes of the ram I think, too, of the dignified gentle patience with which Mr George sits waiting either in his room or on the verandah. When he sees me his face lights up with pleasure, I suppose as mine lit up, as he used to say it did, with happiness, each of us, in the presence of the other.

One memory leads without real sequence to another. My

mother, often quick to voice an opinion or a warning, said at the time when I was ill, unable to keep the fear and the indignation out of her voice, as when I was pregnant for the first time, 'A doctor! And having such an illness. You should have been more careful. With your nursing too you should have known better. You cannot say I did not warn you. Always I said to you to walk on the other side of the road. I taught you to avoid the spots of blood in the snow.'

The cough, when it came, seemed to start somewhere out of reach, persistent and irrepressible. Of course I thought, all the time, of Noël. I actually wished for Noël and Felicity to visit me.

The sputum mugs, with chipped enamel lids, disgusted me. It was not because they were unfamiliar. They were all too familiar. I detested them in the days when it was a part of my work to collect them, empty them and clean them. Describing their contents, either in speech or in writing, disgusted me. And I still detested them.

When I could, when I was allowed to walk about, I looked for places where I could leave unclaimed this terrible ugliness, on a high shelf in the bathroom, in the sluice room or behind the door of the boiler room.

'Where is your sputum mug?'

'I don't have any sputum.'

Hides sputum, was recorded along with my temperature, pulse and respiration.

'A mother has always to forgive,' my mother's repeated words during her visits then.

It is sometimes said that events cannot be transformed into fiction until they are sufficiently over. There will be exceptions. There is too the idea that different elements can be woven together in the creating of characters and story. There can be a merging of the actual and imagined. It is necessary to cultivate the ability to keep the vision sufficiently apart from the real event. It is this ability to hold on to the vision while being involved in the event which helps to bring about the making of a fiction writer or a poet.

It occurs to me now that events are well enough advanced to enable an attempt at this transformation.

It occurs to me too that there are yet more people who have given themselves to me in their several ways, so bringing about changes in me. I am different because of knowing, for example, Noël and Felicity and even that small man, Boris, who visiting one night with his home-made lute, an exact copy of the original, provided a fragile music at the foot of the heap of black slag, the pit mound; a strange ugly place for the serenity of the lute and the self-conscious laughter of the three of them, Boris, Noël and Felicity, as they repeatedly failed to reach the right notes in their singing.

Then there are the widows. Both giving advice and both, in their own ways, giving imitations of attitudes, mainly their own.

My mother's widow and my own widow.

Perhaps this would be a good place to note that I have to acknowledge that my clothes are more suitable for sitting in outpatients' departments than in any other place. I mean, I am never suitably dressed for a restaurant or a concert, a morning or an afternoon-tea party or the waiting room of an accountant or a solicitor – all places for which better and more attractive and fashionable clothes are required. This goes for my consulting rooms too and accounts for the fact that I often wear a white coat there, even though I know the trend (if I can use such a word) is to be dressed in ordinary clothes, perhaps something lacy or knitted, a floral dress obviously home made with puff sleeves or from the current gear, jeans, Reeboks and a T-shirt with a slogan to put patients and their relatives at ease.

EINE BEMERKUNG

Perhaps, as on the previous page, this is as good a place as any for the inclusion of an observation, a glimpse from before, a little explanation, something of that sort.

'Addi,' my mother remarks, 'is fading away in unhappiness.' She adds that this is merely *eine Bemerkung*, and, though it is serious, it can only remain as an observation because it does not do to interfere between married people. She has waited, she says to my father, for the right moment to tell him this.

I am under the table, far back where the table is against the wall. I am trimming the fringe of the green plush cloth with forbidden weapons. I can hear everything. Bert Rose is crying.

Bert Rose, a traveller in fat (mainly for fish and chips), and who grew up in the street where my grandfather, in public, disowned my father for being in prison during the Great War, because he was a CO, has left the room for a few minutes to go to the lavatory. He whistles a small tune when he pulls the chain. I have noticed that people often whistle or sing at this particular time.

Addi, with dark shadows round her eyes and a paleness which, my mother says, is threatening, has left Bert Rose. He has no idea where she is and no idea, at all, why she has gone. Bert Rose cries some more.

Bert Rose and my father are friends. Bert Rose will have seen my father turned out of the house with my grandfather throwing a shilling at him. Bert Rose maintains that my grandfather was only ashamed because of the imprisonment, ashamed that my father was in prison, and not about the reason for his being there.

'Addi is, how shall I put it?' my mother says, '*ein Zigeuner-Mädchen*. You say she has taken her violin? She likes – no, enchanted is better, she is *enchanted* by the *Ziguener*, and the violin, the endlessly sad music of these people. She will be back,' my mother goes on, 'she will come back when the gypsies move on. You will see. In any case,' she adds, 'she will be back for "The Archduke" in the town hall next week.'

Under the table my father's boots are planted on the linoleum. Bert Rose's boots, which are heavier, move and shuffle and I know that his big red hands will be shuffling across his red face as he tries to wipe away his tears.

My father suggests they go on their bicycles to Tinkers' Castle Hill. There is time enough. And Bert Rose says that he has seen a place there where a woman sells eggs and boilers – cheap.

'Bring a fowl and some eggs,' my mother says.

Years later Gertrude, remembering my father and his friend turning up early at her Place that first time, tells me that she feels dreadfully ashamed that morning because, as she tells me, 'I hadn't even washed me when – *there they was* – the two of them, these gentlemen, coming up out of the long grass!'

When she tells me this we are tearing up an old newspaper and wrapping up the new-laid eggs. Black-market eggs, they are called then.

I must explain something about my father. He was always seeing me or other people off at the bus stop or the station. 'I'll come to the train with you,' he'd say at the last minute, just before it was time to set off.

18

His coming to London to see off the boat train is unexpected. Because of this habit of his, it should have been expected. On that occasion Mr Berrington, after consulting his watch, says that it looks as if the train will be leaving on time. He moves his folded raincoat from one arm to the other and holds open the compartment door for my mother and me to climb in. Then he shakes hands with my father. He hopes, he says, that my father will have a pleasant journey back to the Midlands.

'Stay on deck,' my father says to me, 'and then you won't be sea sick.'

As the train begins to move my father walks alongside on the platform. The train gathers speed and my father runs smiling and waving. His white face, anxious and sad behind his smile, is the last thing I see.

I mention Bert Rose because it was Bert Rose who told Mr Berrington that German was spoken in our house. Bert Rose was, at the time, fixing something electrical for Mr Berrington.

Mr Berrington, attracted to the language and its literature, became a regular visitor. He came every Sunday for the midday meal, and he and my father exchanged the texts of the sermons at their respective churches during the first course, and the weather forecast while the pudding was served. Mr Berrington stayed on for his German lesson. Sometimes my mother went to Mr Berrington's house, where his housekeeper provided afternoon tea with sugar bread, which my mother often brought home in a paper napkin in her handbag.

My mother looked forward, always, to the concerts in the town hall. She was accompanied by Mr Berrington. Perhaps it says something for her neighbour, Mrs Pugh (who did not share my mother's taste in music), that she never once commented on the concert going and never once said one word about Mr Berrington's regular visits to my mother's house.

My mother understood that Bert Rose suffered.

'It is in the glance,' she says to me one time later on when

19

we are waiting for a bus. 'It is the glance,' she says, 'the raising of the eyebrows and the small nod – all these – which are so intimate between one performer and another. Perhaps *especially* between the piano and the violin, in the "Kreutzer Sonata", for example. But Addi,' she continues, 'Addi achieves these private and familiar little communications even when there are three players, for instance as in the "Archduke".'

My mother explains the difficulties of different cultural backgrounds. Bert Rose, she says then, holds Addi in reverence but does not understand her.

It is only now all these years later, that on reflection, I am recalling my mother's inability to disguise her surprise and alarm when I tell her, in confidence, that Dr Metcalf is like Levin, the landowner in the Tolstoy novel. This Levin, a nobleman, instead of simply giving orders, takes a scythe and, moving in line with the peasants, he mows his meadows with them. He rests with them and even accepts a share of their simple food. My admiration for Levin because of this, and because of the charming and romantic way he proposes to Kitty, is known by my mother.

'Dr Metcalf reminds me of Levin,' I tell my mother just at the time when I am being drawn irresistibly into the magic world inhabited by Dr Metcalf and Magda. Gertrude, by this time, more knowingly than my mother, is anxiously trying to discourage me from following what she feels is the way to the greatest of disasters.

It is only now as I write this that I begin to understand that my mother would understand and fear for me something which she herself, during her own marriage, had experienced. An admiration and a reverence and a need for a particular person and for whom she was not free.

At that time my seeing Dr Metcalf as being like Tolstoy's Levin did not suggest anything to me about either my mother or Mr Berrington because, naturally, I was not thinking of them. I was thinking only of myself.

And, despite the complication in her own life, it was, without

20

anything being said, clearly my mother's wish that she would, one day, hear the music for the opening of Act III of *Lohengrin* which accompanies the bridal procession of Elsa and Lohengrin to the Bridal Chamber, being played for me. Not liking or even approving of Wagner's music, I think she must have overlooked the fact that *Lohengrin* was one of his compositions.

All this is in the nature of what my mother would call *eine Bemerkung*, a remark, an observation which is perhaps a bit more than a casual remark or a casual observation.

MY MOTHER'S VISIT

'I think it is your half crying, Mrs Wright.' Miss George smiles across the table at my mother who, anxious for her share of the new baby, jumps up immediately making for the door, the hall and the stairs as quickly as she can.

They, Miss George and my mother, decide as soon as my mother arrives to share the new baby, to have a half each, and they take turns to bathe and to change her and to carry her about. My share is naturally the feeding so I get to have an all-night share. Though both Miss George and my mother take a turn each during the one bad night we have had. Colic, they decided together then, and first one and then the other walked up and down with the angry little bundle while I lay in bed, pretending to be asleep, thinking about Mr George and wishing that I could be alone with him. Such a silly wish really.

Everywhere there is the atmosphere of a house being given over completely to childhood. The pram is in the front hall and the baby bath is on the kitchen table. The cradle is moved from one best place to another best place. A fire burns in Mr George's study and the clothes-horse laden with wet baby washing stands steaming there all day and every day. I light the fire there every morning when Miss George asks me to, saying that the weather is not showing any signs of clearing yet. My mother nervously suggests that it always rains, even in summer like this, when there is a new baby. Both women smile at each other.

My mother, it is clear to me, would rather be in her own house with Helena and Rachel. She has been upset by the choice of the name Rachel.

'No one calls a baby Rachel these days. No girl can have this name. Rachel was the Queen of the prostitutes,' my mother manages to say when we have a few minutes alone together.

'Don't be silly,' I tell her. 'That's not true, it's silly, a silly made-up . . .'

'*Im Kloster*', they always said . . . 'In the convent . . .'

It's a Hebrew name I tell my mother. I am reliving an imagined conversation from before Rachel was born. It is a strange experience. 'It's a Hebrew name and it means "like a ewe" and is a symbol of innocence and gentleness. It's a pretty name,' I tell her as firmly as I can, keeping my voice soft at the same time.

Miss George, as usual, with her keen insight, suggests, when my mother returns to the table with the baby in the crook of her arm, held with all the remembered knowledge and tenderness I had seen when she first held Helena, that perhaps when my mother returns home I should go with her, taking the children, for a week.

'That would be very nice,' my mother says trying, in her politeness, not to sound too eager to get to her own place in order to enjoy her grandchildren.

'Thank you, Miss Eleanor,' I say. Later I ask her will she manage alone with Mr George being away.

'I shall manage perfectly,' she replies. 'Life is simpler when one is completely alone. Of course I shall miss the children dreadfully, but a week is only a week, isn't it.'

Mr George is in Europe with a group of students including the un-named one, she of the Bach cantata, trumpet and soprano, laugh. I am at the stage of picturing Mr George and Cantata holding hands secretly during a cultural outing, brushing shoulders and hands accidentally while gazing at portraits of royal princes and princesses and the Emperor Franz Joseph. I manage to picture her – almost immediately, because of her loud cascade of laughter, being forcibly thrown out from the sacred silence of some beautiful and ancient church or from a silent gallery of statues and monuments. This is only a temporary picture unfortunately. I feel certain that Cantata is absolutely stylish in loose artistic unwashed dresses and has her long hair tied back, leaving some strands of hair falling carelessly and deliciously across her unblemished face. She probably calls Mr George Professor or Prof or she might have reached, with the long fingers of a thick-skinned egoist, towards *Oliver*. I have no one to whom I can denounce her.

The postman knocks with an expected package of literary journals for Mr George. There is a letter for Miss George, from Mr George, and a post card for me. I am pleased and comforted at once. It is from Weimar and is a picture of Goethe's *Schlafzimmer*, which has in it the narrowest shabbiest small down-at-heel bed you ever saw. I know at once that he has chosen this especially because of the resemblance to his own narrow shabby bed, his bed which has accompanied him from boyhood and which, he has said more than once, has been transformed for him by Venus into the couch of Adonis.

Goethe must have had another bed, probably a bigger one, because this one is in his *Gartenhaus*. This does not at all spoil the special message the card has for me.

My mother privately calling my new baby *die kleine Vera* or simply *die Kleine* instead of Rachel, says, as we pack to go away for the week, that my father will say that the new baby looks like his mother. This is something, she says, which he always says about a new baby. Even if you brought home a black baby, she says, he would say this. I am pleased to see my mother laughing. Quickly she folds things into the open cases.

Miss George sits in the window seat rocking the baby and singing. Helena is spelling aloud to her from an old-fashioned spelling list on a card. After the spelling she will recite the multiplication tables. Helena speaks as Miss George speaks. Exactly.

'You will never be able to leave them.' My mother, in the train, is suddenly unable to enjoy the peacefulness when both children are asleep. 'They are very kind people and well-educated but they will not let you go. You will be working for them for ever. She will never send you away and you will never feel able to leave him.' My mother cries a bit. 'She sees in you someone who can go on looking after him. People don't ever do things with complete unselfishness. Vera, will you never learn?'

'But where should I go?' I am afraid my mother will not allow herself to enjoy having the children for the week.

'Well,' she says, 'perhaps to study, Vera. Your father and I would be pleased to have the children. Please, Vera let us have the children.'

I tell her then that I am not accepted in Edinburgh for medicine but that I am coming a bit later on to study medicine at my old hospital in the Midlands. I have been accepted there.

My mother does not say anything. Either she thinks I am pretending and making up the arrangement, or else she does believe me and, at the same time, is afraid that the children will remain with Miss George.

We continue the long journey in silence, giving ourselves up to the soothing rhythm of the railway train.

MISS GEORGE'S VISITORS

I have always believed that if you want something very much you will get it.

One of my wishes is granted. Something I really wished for is granted. It is hardly possible to believe at certain times that a wish will come true, but this one does. I do see Miss George, as I always hoped I would, sitting in the window seat half-hidden in the thick curtains, nursing my baby and singing to her in that soft crackling voice which belongs to old age, and is tuneless, and which sometimes disappears altogether even when the person is still singing.

'Where is thy mother, the slut?' Mr George, coming home, bringing a breath of the fog with him, and bending over the pink shawl, says. He strokes the small exposed cheek and the tiny ear with one finger.

'Slut? Ullivar? That is no name for this child's mother, not even in fun or for a nick-name!' Miss George, in her reprimand, shows complete understanding. 'Her name is *Vera*, Ullivar, please remember! And this child is Rachel.'

'*You could tell her,*' I tell Mr George in the evening. But I can see at once that he is thinking of his sister and of his sister's visitors; he is thinking of their hats and their gloves and their thin bread and butter and the wide scalloped tea cups, the fine bone china from which they are accustomed to sip their fragrant tea together in the afternoons. He is thinking of these ladies, of their choir practice and of their Sunday mornings and evenings at the church.

'Miss George always asks me to bring the children in during afternoon tea, to be admired,' I begin to tell Mr George. 'Helena reads from her reading book and draws pictures.' I try to go on to tell him that both children wear the dresses made by Miss George. Helena's has embroidery which is reversible and a ribbon which is pink one side and blue the other, and Rachel's gown is pure white with tiny white embroidered flowers at the neck, the wrists and the hem.

'Miss George really loves them, especially Rachel,' I say. 'And I'm sure she *knows*.'

'I know. I know.' Mr George tells me, as he always does, that he loves me and the babies, both babies. He always calls them 'the babies' even though Helena is already six years old.

In the cherry-wood warmth of the small attic room under the summer-warm gable I cry quietly because I want to be with him all the time. To be *his* and not just on the edge of him and not just now and then. For the present the new baby is mine and only mine, with no questions asked, and having nothing to do with the name of George.

I carry in the heavy tea trays and the visitors admire my children and exclaim over their prettiness and their lovely clothes. Rachel, as the new baby, is passed round as all seem to want to nurse her. As always, I catch sight of Miss George's face, she is full of love and pride and is enjoying herself.

I have to understand that the structure of Miss George's life could never be altered beyond *small* changes which accommodate Mr George.

Miss George has never asked who is the father of the new baby. She is too reserved and well-bred to make an enquiry of this sort.

When I stop crying I feel calmer and, as always, come to the same conclusions. I reach, at a certain point, the thought that there are ways in which I am both fortunate and unfortunate.

One such thought is that Miss George will never ask me to leave. She will never *require* me to leave. I understand too that all people need to be loved and that to have someone to love is perhaps even more important. The only person in the world whom Miss George could love is the one man, her own brother, and she must be her own silent wardress and *not* love him. In spite of their difference in age, or perhaps because of it, the remembered childhood pleasures, the anticipations and the confidences persist in such a way that they cannot be ignored.

Then there is the love, a different kind of love but not all that different from the elder sister caring for the once small brother, the love Miss George has for Helena is another stroke of good fortune. I seem to see, as in a sort of vision, as if my tears have washed my eyes, Miss George, in her apron at the kitchen table carving. Her sharp knife is competent and delicate as she carves judiciously the hot roast, leaving more for cold cuts as being the most economical. Miss George, pausing, holds out the knife to Helena and, from the tip of the blade offers her, in advance, a trembling juicy fragment. An image and a memory to be hoarded.

It is to everyone's advantage that Miss George is amazingly healthy. I imagine her having an athlete's heart beat, unbreakable bones and healthy bowels. It is likely that Miss George could outlive us all. If I look at this supposition calmly, I understand that this can be seen as a disadvantage which seems at times to be, in an unquestionable way, greater than all the advantages.

THE HELPLESSNESS OF
BROTHERS AND SISTERS

'Your father has gone to his sister,' my mother's first words always on a Saturday morning. 'Your father is with his sister.' For as long as I can remember these were my mother's words on Saturdays, a refrain encapsulating the inescapable need for tolerance, a statement, an expression of annoyance bordering on the desperate.

Because of my father's sister, my mother, for the whole of her married life, is not able to stand the sight of a rocking chair.

When I think of my father's sister and of Miss George, Mr George's sister, I understand that there are enormous differences in the ways in which people conduct themselves.

My father stops visiting his sister quite suddenly. After all the years of the Saturdays, of going by train and bus to visit her, he stops going. He never explains to anyone why he no longer visits her house.

When she dies he is required, he says, to go over there, not having visited, for some mysterious reason, for a long time. He is obliged to go, he says, in the event of her death. He is required to clear up her things. His sister, having bought an annuity for herself with what my mother describes as my father's share of the money, does not have any money to leave to anyone.

The sad part about it is, my father says later, that there is a houseful of possessions, furniture, books, pictures, clothes, knives and forks and plates and cups and saucers and photographs, all of which were *treasures* to her but are unwanted by anyone else. He gives away what he can and has to have enormous bonfires for the rest. There is, for example, a whole cabinet of babies' dresses, carefully embroidered, some with smocking, and some trimmed with handmade lace by her girls at school. She has been a sewing teacher at the same school all her life. She was always very proud of the collection of what she called 'my girls' work'. The babies' dresses are, by this time, discoloured and marked in places with iron-mould and mildew; some are actually rotten.

It is this extraordinary coincidence of a special skill which Miss George has, the sewing and the embroidery. Fine sewing and embroidery in particular.

'My girls at school . . .' She, like my father's sister, often starts a conversation relating to something from years ago, about her girls in the succession of needlework classes. 'Some of my girls' work.' Miss George has shown me the cupboard with glass doors in her room. It is full of some of the prettiest things I have ever seen. 'All handworked,' she tells me, when she takes out the table cloths and the tray cloths and the gowns and dresses for babies.

It is years since she retired, so naturally I want to protect her. Perhaps, in spite of what I really want, I do want to protect her and the life she has with her church and her visitors and the people she visits and, more importantly, with her brother.

These Georges, this brother and sister, there is something innocent about them.

There is an indestructible devotion going both ways between Miss George and Mr George. Mr George tells me one time, when we are alone, that it suddenly occurred to him that his sister was the person who had known him for the longest time and that she was the only person who had ever wanted to hear him sing.

I suppose Miss George must have been about thirteen or fourteen when she was left looking after her baby brother.

My father told me that he had to look after his younger sister. Elder brothers and sisters, he said, must always look after the younger ones. He had to take his sister to the elementary school every morning. He was not fond of going to school himself. On one occasion, he said, he returned home telling his mother that the school gates were locked because the school had burned down during the night. This was before his sister was old enough to be taken to school. His mother said she would very much like to see a burned-down school so she put on her hat and coat and walked him straight back down the road to school where the bell was ringing and the children, in their separate playgrounds, were lining up to go in.

In taking his sister to school, my father when telling this would explain, he adopted a method of getting her there as quickly as possible. He hooked an arm round her neck, he said, and set off at a steady trot with her held fast in the crook of his arm, their metal-tipped boots sounding like little horses trotting along the pavement. Sometimes, he said, by accident they kicked and bruised each other's ankles. She wore, he remembered, a round, knitted cap with loose woollen tassels which he could feel against his neck. On arrival at the school he used to push her hard, it was a shove really, through the gate which had an archway marked GIRLS AND MIXED INFANTS in big iron letters. And then he would run off, as if unrelated to her, head down, his responsibility shed, to a similar gateway, arched in iron and marked BOYS.

My father's sister's housekeeper is called a companion. This raises her above the idea of servant. Here at the Georges I am not called a companion. Strictly speaking I am not a house-keeper. Miss George keeps the house and, as the saying goes, she keeps good cupboards. Her household linen is irreproachable and her methods for the care and the upkeep of the rooms are impeccable. I find it very satisfying to be the one to do the cleaning and the washing. I prepare the food, the vegetables and so on, but Miss George carves the meat and makes decisions about what is to be served at the different meals. I enjoy waiting at table when there are guests and, especially I like taking in the laden trays, when Miss George has her visitors for afternoon tea and I hear their little phrases of admiration about Miss George, her room and her tea-cakes. I like to see Miss George happy and she does seem so very happy on these occasions. She never fails, at a certain time during the afternoon, to tell me to bring in the children and there is an added pleasure for me when her guests praise my little girl and my baby . . .

During the week when my mother comes as a visitor Miss George does not have her usual tea parties. It is as if she is, thoughtfully, sparing my mother the sight of me bearing the heavy trays and handing round the cups of tea and the little plates and the lacy table napkins before being told that I can leave the room.

'They will do their own reaching,' Miss George says. It is a little sentence giving me freedom.

My father's sister's companion is a true daughter of the canal barges, sharp-tongued, energetic, quick at mental arithmetic and spelling; she is knowledgeable about things geographical, historical, political, medical and personal. She is a small thin woman with a pile of white hair and a voice. Miss Clayton and my father's sister (my aunt) get on satisfactorily together by frequent repetitions of that certain emotional release which follows on the heels of an all-time, all-encompassing row. These two, they have these rows all the time either when they are alone together or in the presence of company or even when there is simply an audience of one. These rows, violent and at screaming pitch, in an agitation of rocking chairs, come unheralded and end quickly in low-voiced soothing moans and endearments uttered from these same rocking chairs, which gradually subside on either side of the hearth. Sometimes there are accompanying tears.

Once you have cried in front of someone or if you have seen someone cry you are never quite the same with that person again. Miss George has seen me cry. Only once. She was shy and patted my shoulder gently, telling me not to cry. I was scrubbing the kitchen table at the time, and when Mr George, who was mostly the reason for my crying, appeared in the doorway Miss George seemed to place herself between him and me and began to discuss the weather with him even though she had her back to him.

I have seen Miss George cry, though not crying in the way I was, having to sit down by the wet table, holding my face in my hands, unable to stop sobbing.

Miss George lying back, as if still asleep, on her pillows that other morning, when I took her little round tea tray in to her, had her eyes closed and, trembling all along her eyelashes, were her tears. It was that first morning after I had been all night in Mr George's arms in his narrow bed, answering his rather shy response to certain music, music which, he said then, seemed to promise eternal youth.

'This may prove to be purely an intellectual exercise,' he says to me that first time. 'I hope you will not be disappointed,' he says. He tells me I can escape to my own room if I do not want to stay in his. I tell him then that I want him, his nakedness and mine as close together as possible, completely and at once.

The reddish colour of his pullover blends with the suddenly remembered glowing floor boards and cherry-wood furniture of the attic bedroom which I have, for the time being, forsaken and I wonder why, during the wild sweet moments, I should consider this woollen garment and the attic chair, the woodwork of the wash stand and the floor boards.

When, later, Miss George is sorting and throwing out clothes she says the russet pullover is not worth further mending, so I take it. I have it safely with my things. Miss George gives me some of the left-over wool and I darn it and, on cold nights,

I wear it to bed as I used to wear my school hockey jumper for many years.

The tears all along Miss George's eyelashes that morning when she was lying as if still asleep, after the night of the Beethoven quartet, the night when I listened with Mr George, by his fire, to the Beethoven, made me feel that she really knew everything and that it would be right then for us to tell her that we love each other in spite of the great difference in our ages and other insurmountable difficulties, namely because of our different and unbridgeable positions in society. These are not phrases I would use. They could be my mother's if she ever puts this opinion, which she holds, into words. It is something she is sure to do sooner or later when she is upset or angry.

But that time for telling Miss George passes and so do all the other times. Not being able to tell Miss George could become the most important thing in our lives.

Now, when I am either in outpatients' waiting rooms or in my own consulting rooms or on a journey to a conference or, by some miracle, with one or other of my grown-up daughters, the one-time importance, that of being unable to tell Miss George the one thing we needed to tell her, has shrivelled, withered like the limbs of an old man when he no longer walks, or like the shelves of unused crockery and saucepans in a house in which most of the rooms are no longer used, because there are not enough people to sit round the table and no one is requiring well-aired and well-made beds. And perhaps most significant of all, since there is no one to sit in the garden, the garden furniture is actually carried indoors and stored in a room lined with books and where, at one time, the carpet used to be rolled back because the floor was considered to be the best floor for dancing.

Even on the occasion of his sister's death, when all the clearing up is finished, my father does not say what it is that made him stop his weekly visits after going on with them regularly for all those years, in the face of my mother's outbursts of anger and reproach.

My father often says that the people who are the hardest to love are those who need it most. I understand now that he saw his sister as being all alone, unloved, and what is worse, having no one of her own to love. And that is the reason for his journeys every week on the early train, returning at night exhausted after digging her garden or mending something in the house, very often something which should have been discarded and replaced. But what tired him most, my mother would argue, were the tirades of complaints and worries. My mother often remarked that her sister-in-law was like a dog with a bone. She would describe the dog worrying the bone, putting the bone down and taking it up again to shake it first one way and then the other way. She said her sister-in-law would even, like a dog, bury her bone in order to dig it up once more and start worrying it all over again. My father, after one of his Saturday visits to his sister, once asked me what he could suggest she should buy for inexpensive presents for her friends at Christmas because she was worrying about Christmas so much and it was then still only June.

It is only now much later on that I understand why, without saying anything to anyone, he stops visiting his sister. He makes this big change in her life and in his, because of me. A great part of her weekly tirade, for a number of years, would have been about me.

It is like this. I have not seen my father's sister (my aunt) for a long time when she calls unexpectedly to see me. Mr George is at the university and Miss George has taken Helena to listen to the church choir practising.

My aunt would have left home very early for the long journey, several hours by train with buses at either end.

Without touching her tea or the bread and butter I have cut for her she begins to explain in very carefully articulated words that, because of the way in which I am living and *must have lived* (this with a sidelong glance at the baby clothes arranged

37

for airing along the fireguard) she has, in her words, been obliged to cut me out of her will, completely out of her will.

The surprise of this is not in connection with any possible gift being withheld, it is more to do with the fact that she has planned to make this journey for this particular reason, this special intention. The sudden intensification of my own feelings of loneliness is a surprise too. I am already alone. I am accustomed to the idea of being alone, but her words cause an extra emptiness, that of being removed from belonging to a family.

Immediately, perhaps with the aid of a cultivated practice of self-protection, consolation and rescue, without really thinking, I tell her, 'Please don't worry about me, I have been well provided for.'

'Don't tell Dad,' I say later when visiting my mother. The visit is one prescribed by Miss George. Mr George is climbing mountains in the Tyrol with a group of students. Miss George describes me as looking *peaky* and in need of a change of air.

My mother says that it could be considered a great comfort for us both that the Georgian silver teaspoons I am meant to inherit from my grandmother via my father's sister will hang like a great weight round her neck . . . She pauses suitably in her finger-pointing pronouncement, to let all the possible horrors contained in this image be continued in the imagination.

'Don't tell Dad,' I say again, not thinking that of course my aunt would tell him herself, rail at him, have him on the mat, worrying the subject – the dog worrying the bone – never giving him any peace, wanting to know who is providing for me, what sort of people does his daughter know and mix with and what dark world of sin is she being paid to inhabit.

Not thinking, I say again to my mother, 'Don't tell Dad.' She says she won't, but of course she does. As I should have known by then, she always tells my father everything.

And it is after this, though I do not at once make the connection, that he stops going to visit his sister. And I never see her again either.

It is only now while my mind is on sisters, Mr George's sister and my father's sister, I see as *in the lives of the obscure*, that being supplied *first with gilt-edged notepaper and then with baby linen* and hiding out in a large house, remote from my mother and father, my training abandoned and being nothing better than a housemaid is not what she had had in mind for me when I had been earlier safely, as in the promise of Isaiah, graven on the palm of her hand, cherished there and not forgotten. She comes all the way to visit me that day because of all that has gone before and because she is inarticulate and helpless in her inability to protect or even to reach.

WHEELCHAIR . . .
CLOSELY WATCHED ROADS

From Harold Avenue turn left into Hammond turn left into Goldsworthy and almost at once cross over turn right into Bernard going west downhill smooth smooth all the way down into the park. In the park there is hardly anyone about. The slopes of cut grass catch the sunlight and the shade. And the ancient trees, each one a benign sanctuary for the doves, the green parrots and the rosellas, do not change either with the passing years or with the seasons. The plane trees in Hammond and Dunbar have lost their leaves and the bare winter branches on the overcast sky of winter remind me of England and of the cold.

The nape of the neck remains unchanged. The nape of Mr George's neck is not changed. Mr George asks about Miss Eleanor and if she is busy with the children's spelling and their arithmetic. I explain that Miss Eleanor used to be busy like this. He is thinking, I tell him, of earlier times. Mr George says, with his little laugh, that he is sorry for being such a silly old man. I tuck the tartan rug more closely round his knees and remind him that the two little girls are now grown up and that Helena is a cardiologist and that Rachel is an obstetrician. He says he remembers. The wheelchair purrs on smooth smooth on the cement path. Smooth smooth.

I ask Mr George does he remember the night porter at the hospital and his skeleton keys on the small springing hoop which resembles a circular knitting needle. These keys which open everything, all the nurses' rooms, the rows and rows of change-room lockers, the poison cupboards, the operating theatres, the matron's office and the storeroom where the oxygen cylinders are kept. These keys, they open the late pass door to the residents' corridor and the heavy gates at either end of the tunnel which joins the hospital to the Nurses' Home. So many keys. This porter is the one who, in talking about an air raid one night during the war and his wife being alone all night, during the air raid, takes my mind abruptly off the shortage of hair clips to the more important and serious side of the war.

Surely Mr George remembers the night porter who unlocks for us at opportune times years ago.

I ask Mr George if he remembers the Black Country farm and my stupid friendship during the time I am Resident Houseman at my old hospital. And does he remember, I ask, that he wants then to know is it Dr Metcalf and his greedy, ugly wife all over again, and I tell him 'no'; almost to the point of lies, I tell him 'no'. How could he or anyone think of Magda as either greedy or ugly or both.

And does he remember, I ask him, visiting me during my illness and how he stays the night at the Holly Bush one time and travels by Pullman the other time even when my mother prepares and offers a room for him. Does he recall the luxury of the Pullman?

I ask Mr George if he remembers the voyage to Australia when we each take up an appointment together but separately. Does he remember, I ask him, all those shipboard rumours? I mean, I suppose then, that they are rumours. One is the midnight funeral – ceremoniously – but with a secretly insisted upon Union Jack. Then there is the closing of the children's play deck because of a smallpox scare. And then there is the expected, scarcely possible, arrival of a pianist, a violinist and a cellist, a trio renowned for their interpretation of Schubert, being flown out to join the ship for a recital. Does Mr George remember, I ask him, the woman who repeatedly declares she is robbed? Every few days she is robbed of her furs, her dinner dresses, her necklaces and pendants and her Italian shoes, expensive Italian shoes. She is the one, I remind Mr George, wearing a toque, a curious hat which he describes then as a sort of brimless inverted flowerpot. I remind him now that he thinks then that this sort of hat enhances a slightly wicked expression in the eyes.

Then there is the rice-farm widow's well-meaning but impertinent question; surely he does not and never will forget the wording of it.

There is some special quality about the light at a certain time in the afternoons which brings back recurring events and images connected with the particular time of the afternoon, one of these hoarded recollections being the sound of people returning to the house. The afternoon light changing makes Mr George, on some days, ask if Miss Eleanor will be coming home soon.

What are you brooding over, Vera? What are you brooding over in your silence?

On the symptoms of Exophthalmic Goitre, Mr George, on Exophthalmic Goitre.

While the piano music spreads filling the whole room I think of Ramsden, of staff nurse Ramsden, erect beside the polished glass shelves of syringes and needles as she prepares them for the three-hourly penicillin, a long time ago, during the war at the time when train-loads of wounded men arrived in convoy at the hospital. I always tried then to make a point of passing the ward where she was so that I could catch sight of her. It was better when I was able to actually walk behind her and staff nurse Pusey (was that the name?), as they walked, their uniforms rustling, in step with one another, conversing in low voices about books and music and possibly a particular concert which both had been to. Ramsden would be familiar with this particular harmony, she would know the presence of the sound of the neopolitan sixth in Beethoven. I listen for it in the 'Moonlight Sonata', taking my mind off my studying for a few minutes.

What comes after Exophthalmic Goitre, Mr George wants to know when he changes the records. It is the Beethoven fourth piano concerto now, played by Artur Schnabel. How is it possible to think of all the things I must think of during this gentle expanding music.

Your study is more important, Vera. Mr George stops the music even though we both prefer it. I have to think, I tell him, about various things, the circumstance, for example, of a large overdose of insulin or the symptoms of acute spinal meningitis or a description of a normal gastrectomy and then, in addition, a sort of poem to follow; cirrhosis, leucocytosis, orthopnoea, thrombosis, embolism, haematuria, endocarditis, mitral stenosis, erysipelas and uraemia. And then I tell him, there's more, the signs and symptoms for an early diagnosis of Pulmonary Tuberculosis and a close description and recognition of the onset of Anterior Poliomyelitis and then the question how should a doctor deal with a patient who has received a violent blow on the eyeball. Then there's Cyesiology, Cyesis . . .

At least, I tell Mr George, I was not caught out in the exam by diagnosing a woman as diabetic when she was merely pregnant. We knew the trick questions, I tell him, when I was nursing; we knew every year that among the patients presented for diagnosis there would be one normal healthy pregnant woman complete with her 'signs and symptoms' which could appear to be caused by something else.

Can you study, Vera, while we have this music? Mr George wants to know. I tell him that I can. It is not the music which is distracting, I tell him, it is the changing light during the afternoon which makes me think of my mother when she sits, in spite of her next-door neighbour and friend, the railway-man's widow, with *Faust* open on her dining table reading aloud with Mr Berrington whose desire it is to read Goethe in German. My

44

mother and her student are as if caressed together in a shaft of sunlight, which passes slowly from one side of the room to the other as the afternoon goes by. They read aloud, each one reads aloud in turn from the same book, my mother gently, from time to time, correcting Mr Berrington's shy pronunciation.

Galeotto fu il fibro e chi lo scrisse, Mr George says softly, when I tell him of this small picture of which I am, I suppose, the sole custodian. He tells me that these words come from Dante's *Inferno* where Dante is in conversation with two adulterous lovers, Paolo and Francesca. Francesca tells him how the two sat together over an old Romance and then passed from reading to some other pastime. Her words, Mr George explains, mean literally *a pander was that book and he who wrote it*. A pander, he goes on to say, is a go-between, sexually, a go-between. And in the same conversation Francesca makes the famous and much debated statement that there is no greater pain in times of sorrow than to remember times of joy.

'I always thought,' I tell Mr George, putting aside my books and notes for the music and his little bits of conversation, 'I always thought, when I was little, that the telephone was invented on the day when my father tried to make me go into a telephone box to learn how to put the money in and dial a number. It's the same about the hoover.' I go on, 'My mother had her electric cleaner in 1934 and I really thought that was when the first ones were made.'

I suppose it is an old idea that everything starts only with us, with each person, as if nothing was ever known or experienced before. I suppose this is especially true over the discovery of certain music and the disturbance of being in love with someone. I have no idea why I should at this moment remember the field at the end of the street and my father whistling from an upstairs window, at dusk, for me to come home. There is this boy, he is big and old and I do not know where he comes from. He says his name is Victor and I can go bird's-nesting with him.

So I stand in the long wet grass along the hedge, one hedge after another, and this boy is crouching in the ditch. He keeps telling me to move my legs wider and so I try and do this and he is so close under my skirt that I am afraid he will see my knickers. 'Go on,' he says, 'stand wider, you look up above and I'll look down here.' We do not find one nest, not one, and of course no eggs and no baby birds. And then my father is whistling from the back bedroom window, calling me home. 'It's like he's whistling his terrier,' Victor says, grabbing my dress as I twist quickly one way and then the other and make off across the field, running as fast as I can. At the road I look back and there is no sign of this Victor.

The room where my mother sits with Mr Berrington has a french window opening on to a piece of concrete which is meant to be like a small terrace but is concrete all the same. From the concrete there is a path and the lawn, geometrically divided by small flower beds, goes back to a small wild place where there are rosemary bushes and two apple trees, one with cooking apples and the other is the Beauty of Bath, the small, sweet, red-cheeked eating apples.

Whenever I visit my mother, and the weather is fine enough, I sit and read under these trees. Mostly, during the years, it has been reading for my work, the skeletal and muscular structure of the human body and the systems; the respiratory, the vascular, the nervous, the digestive and the reproductive, not for nursing any longer but for my qualifications in medicine.

I have no difficulty, I tell Mr George, in studying either in his house or when I visit my mother's. The only distraction is the distraction of his presence at home when Miss Eleanor and the children are out.

Desire and desire rewarded is a refreshment of both body and spirit, Mr George says afterwards. A pause, *moments musicaux*, he says, and I remind him that this music suffers an inheritance of scorn. Not especially because of the music itself, it being, perhaps, the last private and secret words on the piano from Schubert, but because it is often ruined by people pounding on pianos which need tuning. My mother utters words and phrases which carry her scorn when she hears the neighbours on the other side (not Mrs Pugh's side) play extracts on their awful piano *fortissimo* with all the windows wide open to the freshly cut grass of the small lawns and the sweetness of the summerful herbaceous borders.

Mr George says that Blake was right when he wrote that *Desire gratified plants fruits of life and beauty there*. The neopolitan sixth, he says, in music is matched by these lines of Blake's. It starts like this, he says, *Abstinence sows sand all over Ruddy Limbs and flaming hair*.

The neopolitan sixth, Mr George speaks of it at exactly the right moment, when we are resting against each other and can feel the beating of each other's hearts. My head on his chest rises and falls gently with each breath he takes.

The neopolitan sixth, Ramsden would explain, in her well-bred voice, is a chromatic chord, a chromatic modulation, a slipping from one note in one key to another especially in, for example, Beethoven's Sonata *quasi una fantasia* op. 27 in E flat called the 'Moonlight Sonata', because a critic described part of it once as containing the imagery of a boat gliding over a moonlit lake, possibly the famous Lake Lucerne. The neopolitan sixth being a composer's device which is said to produce thoughtfulness and an emotional, romantic quality of sadness creating pathos involving a listener deeply.

I know that recalling Ramsden in this way, in secret, is the way for me to come back to the ordinary day and the return of Miss George to the house. Sometimes, more often than not, I wonder in what way does Mr George come back into the ordinary things of the household. It is something I do not ask him. I am caretaker, the sole custodian, of all this too.

AN IDIOT SAVANT

'Your father is gone to his sister's,' my mother is standing on her path, her swollen legs hidden in pink and blue cornflowers. She tells me she's made the back bedroom nice with clean sheets and towels and she tells me that my aunt, my father's sister, died and my father, after not going there for some time, a long time, has this feeling that he must go and clear up her things. Miss Clayton, he'd said, was all by herself now, so he must go.

'The back bedroom is all ready for your visitor,' my mother says, 'and I've made up the couch for you downstairs.' I tell her that Mr George has taken a room at the Holly Bush near the station. He has to go back first thing in the morning, I tell her. And I tell her that I'll be staying in my room at the hospital. The Holly Bush is quite near the hospital too. 'I'm operating,' I tell my mother, 'at seven.'

Abbott Abrahams Ackerman Allwood . . . Often as I pass the nurses' dining room on the way to the small dining room which is for the doctors, it is as if Sister Bean, with the register held to her heart, has marched between the tables her voice barking into the silence after someone has hurriedly switched off the wireless . . . Arrington and Attwood. Nurses Baker Barrington Beam Beamish Beckett Birch Bowman D. Bowman E. Broadhurst Brown Burchall . . . If I pause on the threshold of this once familiar place it is almost possible to imagine I can hear the names being called into the reverence of silence commanded by Sister Bean. Though the place holds the memory Sister Bean is no longer here and a register is not called; apparently the nurses objected to having to answer to their names being called. It is a change, a change which would have seemed impossible at one time. The nurses' dining room is full of strange faces and noise. I never hope, in the corridors or the wards, to meet a familiar face, Trent or Lois, for example, or anyone.

In the doctors' dining room, as usual, only Mr Farrer and Miss Wilson are there. Both are reading while they eat and both, as usual, give me the smallest nod and go on with their eating and their reading.

'It isn't a repetition,' Mr George says when I meet him at the station, 'it isn't a repetition, is it, of that fellow Metcalf? This isn't the same sort of thing is it?' Mr George has come all the way from Scotland to the Midlands to ask me this question.

I take him to my room on the doctors' corridor. I tell him, not at all, my friendship with Felicity and Noël is nothing like my friendship with what he calls 'that fellow Metcalf and his greedy wife, Magda'. I tell him of course it is different. I am older now, I tell him. I am a doctor now and in my first resident appointment. I remind him that I am the mother of two daughters and that, above all, I belong to him, Mr George.

'Where would I be without *you*?' I say.

'I don't know that you are any wiser,' Mr George says. 'You are such a strange mixture,' he says. 'An *idiot savant* – perhaps it is that which is so lovable.'

I explain, though he knows from previous tellings, how the hospital was bombed during the war and that the doctors' corridor, the whole wing where we are, had to be rebuilt. It's all so different now, I tell him, it's impossible for me in any way to reach back to a reconstruction of the actual place as it was.

However hard I try, peering at the spacing and the positioning of every door, trying to look beyond the new to the old, I am unable to say which would have been Dr Metcalf's room, the door to Dr Metcalf. I do not tell Mr George that time after time I try, as it were, to put an invisible mark on one of the new doors as if to say *this is the place*, this is where I waited for him, wanting him, and a few times was sleeping with him on the little iron bed which was meant for one person only and was very narrow. But I'm lost in the strange new corridor and am never able to establish where his door was among these new doors.

'As a nurse,' I laugh and tell Mr George, 'I was not allowed to come up here. I did get into trouble because I was seen here by someone who reported me.'

'What does all that matter now?' Mr George says drawing me close. 'Nor does it matter which was that fellow's room. And, if you're sure this other thing, this couple – if I can use such an ugly word – is sufficiently unimportant to you . . .' I interrupt him with kisses.

I am pleased to be a resident at my old hospital, to come back there with a certain status and to have a room on this corridor and to have Mr George as my secret visitor. He is quite right in all he says and his calling Dr Metcalf *that fellow* seems to put him, Dr M., in a suitable place, a place where he no longer, even as Helena's father, matters.

All the same I never ever go up to the doctors' corridor without trying to figure out exactly where Dr Metcalf's room could still exist in all the newness of this part of the building. It is a sort of game with its own ritual of hope and resignation. The second part of the game is a slow walk further along the new corridor which, like the old bombed one, is long. I try to see the moon sometimes at the far end, where there is now a tall window looking across to the wall of the clock tower which is a water tower. The artesian well under the hospital and the power and force of this water supply provided a resilience to adversity and was invaluable during and immediately after the war. At the time of the bomb damage the full moon made a trellis of light and shadow on the opposite wall. It seemed then as if there was a strange room out there, L-shaped, leading to a place shining as a river shines when moonlight lies across the undisturbed water. In spite of tarpaulins and wooden barriers set up then the corridor ended abruptly in space, in a precipice immediately in front of me when I looked, hoping one last time, for Dr Metcalf. The moon then was so wonderfully close I felt as if I could step easily across the gulf straight on to the clean white surface.

When I look at the moon, my father's moon, he always thought of it as his, it is incredible that I was not able then to tell him the small thing I needed to tell. And now for years Helena has run to him, straight into his wide open arms. He has composed a lullaby for her, he makes up stories to tell her and, at times, he cooks a kipper for her over the open fire place. This is something he feels he can do when my mother is not at home. When the kipper is done he holds out the best bits, with the bones removed, on the end of a fork saying to Helena, 'This is the best part. Eat this.'

Even though I am warm in bed next to Mr George, my head resting on his gently rising and falling chest as he breathes in and out in sleep, I think of my father at his sister's place, surrounded by her things, wondering what to do first, and Miss Clayton, alone now, at the tea table pricing the tomatoes aloud when he slices one to eat with his bread and butter.

Why must you always have someone to influence you? My mother's voice is suddenly in my head. These people will only make use of you, this Noël and this Felicity. What are these people? Is what we have here not enough for you on your days off? You are simply looking for a replacement for Gertrude. After all these years and with all your studying you haven't grown up at all yet and *you are a mother* . . . Here I imagine my mother's eyes, cornflower blue matching Helena's blue eyes, filling and overflowing with tears.

It's all a stupid repetition, her voice persisting, it's those Metalcups all over again.

Metcalfs, she always did get the name wrong.

Those Metalcups and their silly selfish wasteful friends and their extravagant and wicked parties. How could you, Vera, these new people, they're using you for their own relationship. And here in my head the tirade has to stop. Relationship is a word not in my mother's vocabulary. My mother would not think to say anything like relationship. This is my own word and it is not exactly mine, I have it from a Lawrence novel in which he uses the phrase a *meaningful relationship*.

'Is all that we have had together nothing now?' Mr George, waking, asks me, interrupting my self-made conversation with my mother. 'Do you forget?' he asks.

'I thought you were asleep,' I say. The room, the Holly Bush room, which I had looked forward to, seems airless in the dark, too full with the double bed and the heavy wardrobe and chest of dark wood. The curtains too are sombre and heavy. Earlier I was pleased because the windows look out over the street which, being near the goods yard of the station is used by the brewers. We lie in each other's arms and listen to a heavy dray being pulled by the Clydesdales. The waggon rumbles over the cobbles and, though I am not looking out now in the dawn, I can imagine the horses and their muscles rippling under their well-groomed coats. Of course it is not possible to talk to Mr George about my new friends, Felicity and Noël. He is nervous of any friendship I might make. His nervousness and subsequent irritation bother me in an indefinable way.

'How can I ever forget,' I say to him and I tell him I want to thank him for making the long journey in order to have a few hours with me. However could I forget that Mr George and Miss George, these Georges, with their softly spoken gentle ways took me into their house after they had locked up for the night and were on their way up to bed themselves. They took me and Helena in, that night, even though they had no idea whether I was a good person or a bad one. They had no way of knowing. Of course I am not able to speak of Noël and Felicity and their strange lives. I can't tell him that when I have time off from the hospital I go straight to my mother's house and, as soon as I can, go on my old bicycle to the little farm. It is, I have to understand, a repetition of my journeys to Gertrude's Place years before. Perhaps all life is, like repeated phrases in music and in poetry, repetition. After all Elke, the au pair at the Georges with the laugh which is a mixture of a pure soprano voice and a trumpet being played triumphantly as in the opening of Bach's Cantata *Praise the Lord in every place*, is a repetition of Hilary who, some years earlier, was the forerunner in Cantata laughter.

'Do you still love *that fellow*?' Mr George asks me, as though he has been lying awake for hours.

'Who?' I ask. I rummage in the half-light for my clothes.

'You know who I mean.' Mr George sits up in bed.

'Which one?' as if there are so many. I know Mr George thinks I am being untruthful. I am tired and worried about being late for the list starting at seven in the general surgery theatre. All night I have been afraid to sleep because of the danger of oversleeping. I am ashamed too because I have not even opened the letter from Helena which is sure to contain crayoned pages from Rachel. I have not even asked Mr George about the children.

'I wish you could stay another night,' I say to Mr George. 'Please stay, will you. Please.' I am dressed and ready to leave. I know it is not possible for him to stay. But I ask him. 'Please do stay.'

I know that Mr George would somehow seem all wrong in my mother's house. It is impossible to imagine him in the bathroom there, and which bedroom would be suitable? And then there are the neighbours. The neighbours would be sure to peer at him. He looks distinguished and this in itself puts him out of place. Even though the flowers in my mother's garden enhance everything they are not quite enough for the reception of Mr George.

I take short cuts to the hospital. I think of Mr George and Miss George, the brother and the sister, and I think of my father and his sister. And then, for some reason, I remember hearing Miss Clayton reading one long light summer evening, long ago, when I was upstairs in bed. I was still at school then and visiting for a weekend. Miss Clayton was reading aloud to my aunt;

> When she rises in the morning
> I linger to watch her;
> She spreads the bath cloth underneath her window
> And the sunbeams catch her
> Glistening white on the shoulders,
> While down her sides the mellow
> Golden shadow glows as
> She stoops to the sponge, and her swung breasts
> Sway like full-blown yellow
> Gloire de Dijon roses.

'It's you, Miss Daisy,' Miss Clayton screams her interpretation. 'It's you, Miss Daisy, swilling yourself down in a basin.' She reads on;

> She drips herself with water, and her shoulders
> Glisten as silver, they crumple up
> Like wet and falling roses, and I listen
> For the sluicing of their rain-dishevelled petals
> In the window full of sunlight
> Concentrates her golden shadow
> Fold on fold, until it glows as
> mellow as the glory roses

Miss Clayton reading as the moon comes up the summer evening sky, reading Lawrence to my Aunt Daisy in her own voice and accent with the sing-song tones of the canals, her voice rising at the end of every line.

'It's *you*, dear,' she screams, sending her pleasure and

55

excitement up through the house. 'It's you, Miss Daisy! *You* having a camper's *bath*!' Her voice vibrating singing up at the end of every phrase and the 'a' in bath short and sharp, lemon sharp, as in the north and in the Midlands, this short 'a' considered by my mother to be both ugly and *common*.

'It's a luverly po-emm, Miss Daisy, it's a luv po-emm, it's *ever so nice*,' Miss Clayton shrill with the delight of the portrait of love and the warmth and stillness of the summer night approaching. 'Oh Miss Daisy, it's ever so nice in't it. *It's like a painting.*'

I think of my father visiting unknowingly this adoration of the rose, this Gloire de Dijon, this expression of beauty and love. And then if I think about it, there is the *meaningful relationship* as in the Lawrence novel but without all those stockings, a defiance of red, of coral and canary, Lawrence's stockings – perhaps without any thought about the legs to go in the stockings. I start to think and wonder about my aunt's legs and Miss Clayton's. It is as if they never had any legs all through the years. My own stockings, like Miss Clayton's and my aunt's, are black.

The short cuts seem longer as if I had lost the way. The early morning, with the long day ahead, is inhospitable. Without sleep I am afraid I shall not manage the day. This is a raw and unkind time for parting. I have seen other people, at times, having an early morning unhappy cup of coffee, before parting for the ordinary things in their lives after being secretly together for a few stolen hours. I do not want to be a part of this.

Mr George, alone in the dingy hotel room, will have to get dressed and wait alone at the station before his train leaves. When he said he would walk back to the hospital with me, I told him no, he'd make me late. I told him I'd have to run all the way and that I did not want to leave him having to walk back, his face pink in the cold and his eyes watering because of the wind. I'd feel conspicuous I told him, unkindly, having to part in the street like that. And then knowing he was walking all the way back to the Holly Bush. Alone and with the dreariness of being up and dressed too soon.

In the scrubbing-up room Farrer and Wilson are already gowned and waiting. They comment, with eyebrows raised above their masks, on the dark circles round my eyes and they make little amused remarks about what they describe as my rough *night on the tiles*. Both of them, it seems to me, have nice eyebrows. It is the effect of the eyebrows arched above the white cotton which is so striking.

'How many times?' Farrer asks.

'Seventeen,' I say, and I turn off the special taps with my elbows.

THE HOUSE STANDING OPEN TO THE SPRING

Whenever the sun shines, even if it is only a pale and fading sunshine, my mother opens her front door and as many windows as she can. She calls it 'the house standing open to the spring', even if it is some other time of the year.

Her cornflowers remind me of other cornflowers, just as when her garden is full of pinks and peonies and roses I think of other times when these were in profusion.

'Why do you always have to have some other place to go when you come home for a day off from the hospital and why always a couple?' My mother's indignation shows between her shoulders as she bends over the sink. 'Have you forgotten already how easily people make use of you? And what is it about these people? This couple?'

'Felicity prides herself,' I tell my mother, 'on being able to make a shepherd's pie and bake a cake in the time it takes to listen to Beethoven's ninth symphony on the wireless.' I tell my mother she would like Noël, Felicity too, they are both cultured people. 'I think they would like *Faust*,' I tell her, hoping to please her.

The black-out shutters in the hospital, where I was nursing during the war, were put up every evening so that light would not show from the large building. Before the war with all the windows lit up, the hospital, it seemed to me, looked like a great ship forever in harbour. Two porters put up the shutters at night and another two took them down in the mornings. The evening porters started on chests on the fifth floor and worked their way down both wings of the hospital, through obstetrics, gynaecology, ear, nose and throat, orthopaedics, the private medical wards and the private surgical and so on. Because it was such an immense thing to get done they had to start about four-thirty, when the afternoon sun was pouring into the wards. So, it was like this, coming off duty at half-past five for an evening off before my day off; the sudden light evening outside, after being in the darkened ward, was a surprise to say the least. This forgotten unexpected light – it was something which lifted me from my tiredness then – this summer evening queening it still through the city and the suburbs, I could not get enough of it. I always sat upstairs in the bus, on the left, so that as we lumbered through the suburb, scraping the summer-green leafiness, it was as if I was right there in these green tossing trees for the whole journey.

As I sit now on the top left-hand side of the bus I feel, as I did then, the pleasure of the summer evening – having come from the artificial light of the closed-in general surgery theatre in the same hospital where the black-out shutters used to be put up every afternoon years ago. Other memories follow out of sequence, the red cabbages on my father's allotment and how he left cabbages as gifts on the doorsteps of unknown neighbours in the street, the roan horses on the tow paths pulling barges laden with coal, and a gypsy who cursed the veins in my mother's legs causing her the inflammation of the veins which she suffers from now.

Perhaps it is the Regency tea party which is uppermost in my mind with its promise of Queen Anne cups and saucers, hand-embroidered napkins, China tea with cream and yards and yards of chiffon . . .

'You must come,' I tell my mother. But she is too shy to visit my new friends.

'There's going to be chiffon, you know, lovely light thin gauze, draped along the mantelpiece,' I start to explain. But she continues to shake her head saying she couldn't possibly.

'It's going to be Regency,' Felicity says, every time I go over there, bunching the light material in her capable hands. 'Do bring your mother.'

My mother is unable to trust these two, Felicity and Noël. She has this feeling of mistrust without even meeting them. Perhaps it is my enthusiasm for them which worries her and the fact that, as soon as I arrive home for my time off, I go at once, on my bicycle, to their place. I admire their knowledge of music and literature and their ability to conduct whole conversations in another language or within quotation marks.

'*Suffering is like art we create it within ourselves . . .*' Noël says. 'Strindberg.'

'Look,' says Felicity, 'at *the ruin of the individual when he isolates himself . . .*' Noël says, 'Strindberg again.'

They have the ability to turn a serious conversation or discussion into something apparently ridiculous and light hearted, changing their voices and their words, using words like *perchance* and *I pray you, methinks* and *forsooth*. Or, they adapt the language from Shakespeare's stage directions, *exit running, attendants follow, exeunt severally, a trumpet sounds and trumpet answers within.*

Both have been to Oxford, they speak of Balliol and other colleges with an affectionate familiarity which is enviable. When I ask them what it means to have read Greats they explain that they have studied ancient Greek and Latin, ancient history and ancient and modern philosophy. 'You will have had your beginners' books in medicine – surgery, obstetrics and psychiatry – just as we have had ours in our subjects,' Noël says.

Felicity's dark grey Oxford flannels are mostly hidden under coloured aprons. Noël is fragile, they tell me, and that is why they have this house in the field. He has a cough, I notice, and is always hungry, ravenously. Noël is the brilliant and sensitive one, Felicity says. Noël, according to Felicity, maintains that unless a scholar has had a classical education there were many writers whose work would remain obscure. He is, Felicity says, interested in Eliot's obsession with Heraclitus and Virgil.

'I'm afraid all this is above my head,' I tell Felicity. And Noël says then that he suffers from the illuminated intelligence which sick people have. And then they sing together as they often do in the middle of a conversation, as if they are characters in an opera.

> *Den Adigen steht die Ehrenhaftigeit*
> *im Gesicht geschrieben.*
> *Nun, verlieren wir keine Zeit*
> *augenblicklich will ich dich hieraten*

'A *nobleman's honour*,' Felicity explains the meaning, '*is written in his face. Now, let's not waste time. I'll marry you.*' When Felicity laughs, a tenor voice seems to sing through the well-bred laughter. Their voices, when they sing, are pure and able, sustained as if with deeply felt and understood tenderness and love, as if nothing could go wrong with either of their voices or with them or with me.

They introduce me to the plays of Ibsen. They like to read plays aloud, taking the different parts themselves. In *The Wild Duck* they make me read Hedwig because, they say, I am like her.

When my father asks me one time on my days off, 'Have you got a nice book? What is that you're reading?' I show him the book and I tell him I'm reading *The Wild Duck* and how Ibsen is showing his audience how we all have a lie to live by and that it is wrong to take away a person's life lie and put nothing in its place.

'We should all be completely honest,' my father says. 'No lies.'

'It isn't exactly a lie,' I try again, 'it's more like a mask.' My explanation does not seem very clear; I leave it like that, though I feel my father would be interested in the ways in which Ibsen uses lampshades to show things about his characters, Hedwig's approaching blindness for one thing. And how his characters talk about one thing, meaning something else at the same time. I resolve to listen more carefully when Noël and Felicity read.

'These people,' my mother says, 'are arty crafty.' How do they earn a living, she wants to know. And how do they pay their rent? Decrepit as the place is they would not get it for nothing. 'They must get money from somewhere,' my mother says. Her silence after this remark suggests something evil in the lives of my new friends. My mother, being forever unsure of her own place in a society to which she has never managed to become accustomed, bases her attitudes and opinions on those of a neighbour, a railway-man's widow, Mrs Pugh, who is a dressmaker. Crawling round on the floor with her mouth full of pins while she adjusts a wayward hem, this neighbour, it seems to my mother, knows all there is to know about human life and how it should be lived.

'You don't never get no pleasure,' the neighbour tells my mother often. And when the New Odeon Cinema reopens on the edge of the housing estate they, in out-of-date beaded dresses made by Mrs Pugh, go to the pictures together, twice a week, when the programme changes. They sit in the warmth in the rich golden splendour of gilt-edged mirrors, thick carpets, gold-brass light fittings, chandeliers, every one with a hundred little bulbs shaped like candle flames, gold-brass handrails, palm trees in polished brass pots and voluminous red velvet curtains making secluded alcoves where patrons can rest after an emotionally exhausting film. In the interval they listen to the theatre organ as it rises from its cave in the floor. Often there is the rambling nostalgia of music from the war years, a medley of tunes from 'The White Cliffs of Dover', 'Room Five Hundred and Four', 'Roll Out the Barrel' and 'Knees up Mother Brown'.

My mother observes often that the theatre organ is versatile. Mrs Pugh and my mother also order afternoon tea which is brought to them, as in pre-war days, by maids in black dresses with white aprons and caps, afternoon tea with dark fruit cake on little trays, which look, my mother declares, like hand-beaten silver.

So when my mother agrees to accepting the invitation to the Regency tea party it is on condition that Mrs Pugh can come too. They will catch the two o'clock bus and walk from the corner and I am to meet them at the field path.

It is true, they, my two new friends are artists. One of them makes a skirt for me from cloth woven by them both. Knowing how long weaving takes, a skirt length is indeed an enormous gift. Between them they are always giving me presents, something made by themselves. They, as well as calling me Hedwig, call me Persephone.

'Persephone!' one of them calls, when I am trying to ride my bicycle over the tufts and crevasses in the field. 'Persephone, harbinger of spring and bringer of destruction, what have you brought for us, have you been to the shop?'

They are always hungry and if I bring cake made by my mother they fall on it, as they say, like wolves. They make things, bookshelves, pottery dishes, egg cups, cloth – 'But all uneatable,' Felicity says. 'Bring some bread with you next time, we have lovely home-made jam.'

They rent the place. It is one of those dilapidated farm houses remaining partly in ruins, in a small triangle of green meadow right in the middle of an industrial area which has grown up all round it. To one side is a coal mine and a brickworks and on the other side is the bone and glue factory. Rising immediately behind the house is an ugly slag heap, partly overgrown with coarse grass and coltsfoot. The meadow is low lying and enclosed by hedges of hawthorn and elderberry. There is a derelict wash house to one side of the kitchen door and next to this is a potter's wheel and a kiln built by themselves. They have a cow and some hens.

'Persephone,' they say the first time I eat something there, 'now you will have to stay with us!'

'But I can't stay,' I tell them, 'I have to go back to the hospital. I'm operating at seven in the morning.' That is all right, they agree, I can be part of the time at the hospital and the rest of the time with them. 'That way it will not be hard for your mother to find you.'

My mother, knowing all too well every time where I am, asks me about Mr George. She wants to know what he thinks about my going there. And shouldn't I be saving up my weekends or other days off to have them together so that I can make the journey to see how my children are. What kind of mother am I that I can take work so far from my children. I tell her that I am arranging for the children to visit during the school holidays. Miss George will bring them herself and travel back the same night by Pullman. This pleases and comforts my mother and she says that Miss George could stay overnight and I say, well you know Miss George, she will want to get back to Mr George. 'You might have told me your arrangements, Vera,' my mother says. 'I know you need friends, Vera,' my mother says in a softer tone and I know that she has it in mind to choose some material, so that Mrs Pugh can make some dresses for Helena and Rachel in readiness for the visit.

Scrambling on the slag heap with a trowel and an old cricket bag we, Noël and Felicity and I, collect bits of poor quality coal from the black scree of waste. They have to have a coal search every day.

One day I find a cucumber in the road. 'I got off my bike,' I tell them, 'right in front of a tram to pick it up.' I find their pleasure and excitement over the cucumber touching. Felicity makes sandwiches which we eat, without washing our hands, out on the slope of the ugly pit mound.

It is not a long ride from the housing estate where my mother and father live to the farm. Because of them, Noël and Felicity, I seem to notice things more. They call it 'being aware'. They say it is not because of them. They say it is because I am 'that sort' of person. I like this idea very much.

To go to the farm I ride my bicycle along the main road, where I often have to wait on the left of a brewer's dray to let people on or off a tram. The Clydesdale horses stand waiting, tossing their noble heads.

Going off the main road are quiet roads lined on both sides with the narrow terraced houses built for miners and railway workers. Their front doors, all with white donkey-stoned doorsteps, open directly on to the pavements. Every now and then, in between the jostled streets and houses, there are fields and hedges and some old farm buildings left over from earlier times.

When I first went there, that first time, it was in February. I stopped to peer through the hedge, remembering a family which had lived there when I was a child. I often walked with my mother along this road when we came home by train. Once, there were spots of blood in the snow alongside the winter-thin hedge. My mother, frightened of the illness, told me to cover my nose and mouth with my handkerchief. She said then to always walk on the other side of the road. We crossed over.

Another night when I was walking home with my mother we heard someone crying in the darkness ahead. There was a sharp fragrance of elderberry; my mother said it helped to hide the dreadful bone and glue factory smell. My mother called out to ask who was crying. We stood still in the middle of the road and, after a bit, a girl came out from the black patch which was the elderberry. She cried and told my mother she was Sylvia Bradley and her father had turned her out with only a shilling. We walked on together, all three of us, slowly. The smell of the bone and glue was stronger as we left the elderberry behind. With a heaving roar the blast furnace on the other side of town opened and the sky was red with the familiar glow. We heard the wheels at the mine shaft turning as one lot of miners went down the shaft and the other lot came up. Sylvia Bradley cried, saying she had nowhere to go.

My mother, who never let us play with the Bradley girls, tried to comfort Sylvia. She said to her to go home again and that when her baby was born everyone would be sure to love the little newly born child. 'You will see,' she said then, 'they will not turn you out. Go back home to them. They will love your baby,' she said.

Some time later on Emily, another of the Bradley girls, came with a shabby pram to collect some clothes my mother had put ready.

It is while I am parting the hedge that day to look through at the old farm buildings that one of them, Noël, calls to me to come in. Their kitchen that day is warm and sweet with apple jelly. The shining jars are still warm. On the table there is a little heap of red-and-blue-checked gingham covers cut round with pinking shears to go over the jars when they are sealed. Felicity, dripping hot wax on each jar, explains that they made the jelly with apples stored from the autumn. 'Wrinkled winter apples,' she says.

The February day is soft and mild and Noël, for my first day, writes the first line for a poem on a bit of paper,

The February night, the warmth the stillness

and gives it to me as we all three walk in the dark, me pushing my bicycle, as they accompany me part of the way home.

My mother feels certain that Noël and Felicity are in hiding. 'They're hiding from something, those two. Why don't you keep away from there?' She says she'll speak to my father. I know she will because she always tells him everything. She says she'll telephone Mr George but I am not so sure that she will.

As the day for the Regency tea party draws near I am anxious about the dirty state of the house. They seem to enjoy writing their names and audacious remarks in the dust. They leave unwashed plates and clothes everywhere and they never make their bed. They say that because the bed is so big, taking up all the space in the bedroom, they can't get round it to make it. I despise myself really for wanting to impose my suburban and hospital-trained standards on them. And especially I despise myself for buying a lavatory brush on the way there one morning. They never seem to notice that anything needs cleaning.

The little piece of meadow, left over, brings some prettiness as the seasons change. There are daffodils, the flowers of the hawthorn, the pink and white mayflowers – unlucky, Mrs Pugh says to bring into the house, but Noël and Felicity laugh at that when I warn them. Then there are the buttercups and the daisies and, on the slag heap in patches, the sturdy yellow coltsfoot. There are wild roses in the hedges and the flowers heralding blackberries and then the glistening fruit itself and, at last, the hawthorn berries, elfin bunches of autumn, and then the rosy wild apples, crab apples. There is something magical in coming upon a corner of the earth like this in the middle of the smoke and dirt and the night-time roar of the iron and steel works when the sky is glowing hot red, red orange, from the opened furnaces. And then there is the unforgettable noise of the wheels turning as the miners' cages are going down or coming up. And then the times of quietness between all this. Sometimes a stillness as of a smooth lake and a quietness, unbelievable.

'Don't they speak nice,' the railway widow, Mrs Pugh, is not able to hide the approval in the face of her disapproval and distaste. She stands with my mother, both of them balancing in their best shoes, on a tuft of grass at the edge of the mud. My mother, as a rule, looks up to and admires people, who, having been to Oxford, speak with that special resonance as certain vowel sounds are brought down through the nose, as if an 'n' lurks somewhere within these words. The short 'a' offends her, it is a kind of curse to be got rid of. She is quick to correct people, even strangers in shops. She approves of the dark grey Oxford mixture, the special cloth for the flannels, and the Oxford sandals saying that they are elegant, one of her favourite words, and go well with that special haircut which allows a heavy, if drab, wave to fall across an intellectual forehead.

The only trouble about their clothes is that when my mother and Mrs Pugh arrive, my two friends are not wearing any.

Nervously I stand with the two visitors listening to the high-pitched little screams which belong to the way in which my friends talk and laugh. The smoke from the wash-house chimney rewards us with a sudden shower of sparks and soot. From inside comes the sound of a tin bath being shared.

'Always, but always, the accomplished acrobat. Not a muscle out of place. You delightful tormenting creature!' A laughing well-bred voice causes the visitors to look away from each other and to stare stonily at the generous surrounding of mud.

'Acrobat! Contortionist!' The two-toned laughter contains in its music the sounds of an exchange of playful slappings of wet hands on wet bare flesh.

'And whose little bottom is this?' Slap slap. 'And whose little bottom is this?' Two more slaps.

'Who or what are these so-called friends of yours?' My mother's white hat, with its small spotted veil, is an inadequate protection.

'Them forrin or what?' Mrs Pugh jerks her head towards the wash house.

'They're Bohemians,' I say.

'It's not a question of which country.' My mother's lips are in a thin pale line. I look away from her.

'Bohemians,' I try once more. 'You know,' I say, '*A la Boemm*, as in art, in painting and poetry, that sort of thing, clay modelling, pottery.' I wave a hand towards the kiln. Another high-pitched scream and a laugh interrupt my attempt.

'Well,' Mrs Pugh says, 'I can't say as I know much about

art but I like a nice picture now and again, you know sumthink pretty, flowers or a nice bowl of fruit or a sailing ship.'

One of the inmates of the wash house has started to blow bubbles. The other is singing in that surprising voice, a voice full of feeling. I recognise the descent, Leonora's descent, the faithful wife going down into the dungeon. The singer changes character and, beginning with the penetrating cry to God from Florestan, gets as far as *O schwere Prüfung* before breaking into shrieks of laughter.

'Sounds like there's two of a kind in there,' Mrs Pugh purses her lips.

'Really!' My mother's speech ends as the wash-house door is pushed open and two figures, incompetently sharing a bath towel, step on to the plank which partly bridges the mud between the wash house and the kitchen. The two of them fly across in a flurry of pink nakedness.

'I'm going for the bus even if I have to stand and wait the whole two hours for it out there on the corner.' My mother begins to pick her way across the sodden meadow. 'They'll wreck your career, those two.' There are tears in her voice. 'Believe me,' she says, 'between them, those two, they'll wreck your career.'

Unable to look at my mother's white hat, I take her arm to steady her across to the next little island of turf. This is the second time that I am seeing myself quite plainly. That first time I was working my way through bladders and stomach ulcers, gall stones and various surgical conditions, through the men's private wards and the women's private wards, a never-ending path to being a battle axe of a sister in charge of some God-forsaken place like Radium Therapy or the diet kitchen on the Lower Ground Floor, or worse, in charge of the ear, nose and throat theatre, with its two humourless and untender surgeons, always at war with each other, and on to the final triumph, that of being a District Nurse, enormous in navy blue, on a bicycle, visiting patients, admonishing husbands and delivering babies on sheets of newspaper in overcrowded kitchens or bedrooms. Not knowing then that I was being, in the eyes of my mother, wrecked, I went forward towards the consequences, being rescued at the same time. Now a second wrecking or rescuing is in the tears on my mother's soft, carefully powdered cheeks. On a different level, a life of supra-pubic catheters and septic toe nails waiting to be removed and the decision to make between obstetrics and gynaecology, general surgery, third-rate psychiatry or general practice is ahead of me. I notice once more my mother stepping carefully to avoid spoiling her patent-leather shoes. I can hardly bear to look.

'I won't let them. No!' I say, 'No, I won't let them. I won't let anything wreck . . .'

Before my mother can bring out the words, 'It's that Dr Metalcup all over again,' Felicity, dressed, as usual with a red-checked apron over the grey flannels, calls to us to come indoors. The kettle is boiling and the tea will be ready in a minute.

My mother and Mrs Pugh, with customary good manners, hesitate.

There isn't any chiffon and the cups and saucers are absolutely not Queen Anne. Even though I have never seen Queen Anne china, I know the tea cups are simply the usual ones, white with a thin gold line on the rim and a shamrock, a kind of trefoil or clover, in gold, at the bottom of the cup. Everything just ordinary. Felicity must have discarded the chiffon and the Regency idea.

Noël and Felicity, their wet hair brushed back behind their ears, are charming and wait on my mother and Mrs Pugh with gentle movements. The kitchen is warm. They must have pulled out all the dampers, the fire in the stove is roaring, burning up all the carefully scrounged coal. An unaccustomed extravagance.

'Thank you very much, ta.' Mrs Pugh holds her cup and saucer high, level with her proud bosom. 'Well, thank you very much, I don't mind if I do.' She helps herself delicately to the bread and butter from Felicity's offered plate.

During the tea time I go outside and, crouching in the rain which has started, I plant out a few cornflower seedlings. I use a wooden spatula of the kind used for pressing down the tongue during an examination of the throat. I keep it in my pocket along with my watch, a small scalpel and my old nursing scissors. These things, together with my pen are my instruments. I cherish them and hope to add a number-eight catheter when one in good condition turns up. This habit of keeping equipment belongs to the war years. All kinds of essential things are forever in short supply. Doctors and nurses hide them. I have no idea, while I am working with the little plants in the mud, that the possibility of a number-eight catheter could ever cease to be of importance to me. I think of the surprising show of colour the little seedlings will produce later on, and it occurs to me that, up to the present time, I have made remarks and carried out various actions, both simple and complicated, always without looking ahead to consequences surprisingly pleasant or otherwise. And that one of the aspects of both sowing and planting is that it is necessary to remember that the work is done with hope. While I am crouching there close to the earth, feeling the cold rain make its way round the collar of my old coat, another thought comes to me. Never once has my mother reproached me over my lack of a *good* marriage, as she would hope to think of marriage. Perhaps my mother, seeing me living safely and well with the Georges, is too polite, too aware of what might be impossible, to ask outright, 'Why doesn't Mr George want to marry you?' and, 'Why is there no marriage since there is now the second child?' For some years (Rachel is now seven years old and Helena almost twelve), she has been seeing me remaining as the maid at the Georges. She has been an onlooker during my years of study carried out during this time of my *maidship*. And she has been looking on while I am, at the same time, *mother*, providing Miss George with a longed for, perhaps secretly longed for, rôle which, I suppose, should be my mother's and which I know she wants very much in spite of gossip among neighbours. It comes to me then, with considerable surprise, that this mother I have, this mother being forced into the position of onlooker, possibly knows, understands even, that Mr George and I are lovers whenever there is an opportunity for us to be alone together. In spite of thinking this I am, in reality, unable to imagine that she would ever think about such an idea. And, of course, at present she is being forced to watch with an understandable fear (which I am ignoring) my friendship with Noël and Felicity which, because of limited free time, is intense.

A small scene returns often when I am alone, like now in the mud with the tiny plants. It is the day when I leave the Georges, qualified and about to go to the train in order to travel back to my old hospital, not as a nurse this time but for an appointment as a doctor and to be known as the Resident Surgical Officer – R.S.O. for short. Elke is coming in through the front gate. The hedge of sweet briar is sparkling with rain drops after a recent shower. My two little girls are with her, they have been for their walk. All three have wind-reddened cheeks and bright eyes.

Elke, seeing me standing with the Georges on the rich colours of the mosaic in the porch, in that safe place between the storm doors and the delicate stained glass of the front door, calls out, 'Ha! The rescued maid leaves Saint George and the Dragon.' And, with her second-hand cantata laugh resounding she brings the children up the path. I kiss them both, one last time before I leave . . . for the time being . . .

For the time being I have to remember that the sun-warmed floor boards and the cherry-wood furniture in the attic rooms at the Georges are not mine any longer. Elke will have unpacked her rucksack there. A young woman comes in daily to be at Miss George's elbow during the little ceremonies of carving or serving afternoon tea, and to care for the rooms with duster and polish in addition to the special soap and hot water for the stone flags in the hall and in the kitchen.

'Did you see the ankles and the collar bones of the one of them?' Mrs Pugh says, in the field, on the way back across to the bus. 'I never did see the size of them, not on a woman anyhow, and not on Mr Pugh neither, but then,' she pauses, 'Mr Pugh, he was a small man.'

My mother seems to be absorbed in keeping her feet as dry as possible. I walk to the bus with them pushing my bicycle with one hand in the centre of the handlebar, something I have seen my father do with ease but which proves hard for me, and holding my mother's arm with the other. Feeling her arm tense inside her coat makes me long to be close to her, to tell her I am sorry.

'A good cup of tea,' Mrs Pugh allows, 'for all that it was China.' And then a fresh thought, 'China tea! What with the expense of it, *them* having China tea!'

I hope my mother will make some remark about the fragrant cup of tea, one of her phrases, but she remains silent. 'A course to my way of thinking China's nothing as good as real.' Mrs Pugh has the last word.

During the afternoon tea, Felicity and Noël, I can see, are contrite about their late bath. The water will have taken too long to heat. I do not need any explanation from them.

At home my mother, because I have not had tea, makes bacon sandwiches for me, using up all the bacon.

'For you to eat in the train,' she says.

Instead of going to the station I go quietly round the side of the house to the shed and, taking the bicycle as quietly as I can, I ride off in the dark, without a lamp, to the farm.

There is a small car on the grass at the edge of the mud. There has never been a car there before. I hesitate. The smell of crushed grass mingles with petrol fumes.

'Persephone! What a surprise!' Felicity opens the door to reach for some coal. 'Shouldn't you be at the hospital?'

'Come in. Come in,' Noël calls from the kitchen. 'What

destruction do you bring? Anything to eat? Any victchooalls?'

I tell Felicity that, yes I should have gone back but I want to thank them for the afternoon. And, in any case, I am too late now for the train.

Felicity, insisting that I stay the night, introduces me to their visitor, someone I have never seen there before.

'Boris, this is Persephone.' Boris, they explain, makes or rather recreates ancient musical instruments. He has with him a fourteenth-century lute which he is going to play and Noël and Felicity are going to sing.

'A replica only,' Boris says, looking modest.

I explain that I should confess to knowing nothing about the lute. No one pays any attention to what I am saying, but I persist in trying to tell them that I do not know the lute.

Boris plays his lute and Noël and Felicity, after a few false starts and much laughter and coughing, sing. Boris eats all the bacon sandwiches saying that being registered as a vegetarian, in college, means that he never has any bacon. Why don't Felicity and Noël keep a pig, he wants to know. He wipes his fingers on his little black beard.

'Your beard, Darling,' Noël squeals between coughs, 'is positively charming, exquisitely *pubic*.' Boris bows and plays some more music and the other two sing some more. I feel excluded but smile and applaud. I am wishing I had not come back. I think of my warm bedroom at the hospital. During an interval in the music making, while Boris drinks Noël's supply of prescribed stout, I tell them I ought to be getting home.

'Why?' Noël says. 'They do not know you've missed the train.'

'That's true,' I say, wishing at the same time that I had not said it.

Felicity digs about in the small cupboard under the stairs and pulls out two blankets and a pillow.

'You'll have to be up for the early train,' she says. Upstairs in the little back bedroom I discover that both blankets and the pillow are damp. The scree of the ugly slag heap rises directly outside the small window. I am all too aware of the blackness which blots out any light or glow in the night sky.

I am so cold in bed. I nearly go downstairs to the fire to tell them that I've changed my mind, that I'll go home after all. I have this extraordinary thought that in a moment I'll change and be their equal and, with my explanation, escape will be simple.

Every now and then little bursts of well-bred conversation and high-pitched screams of laughter reach me, where I am lying shivering under the inadequate covers. I have never stayed here for a night before and it seems to be the silliest thing I have ever done.

'Has the sanatorium caught up with you yet?' Boris's voice is abrupt in the middle of the laughter.

There is a sudden silence and Felicity replies in a low voice, 'Not yet.'

'I see you've a new *messenger*. Does *she* bring in the goods as satisfactorily as Jules did?'

'Don't, do *not* mention Jules,' Felicity snaps.

'Oh, Jules,' Noël yawns. 'Jules let us down badly. Very badly.'

'I take it,' Boris says in a light and playful way, 'there was nothing in it, as usual, as there usually isn't for the Jules of this world. I think I said, didn't I, that Jules would be bound to let you down sooner or later.'

'It was sooner rather than later,' Noël says.

'Well,' Boris says, 'as usual you have found someone else, though her accent is *appalling*, someone else to bring in the bacon. Oops! pardon the pun, darlings.'

I lie there listening to their huge and artificial laughter and, in my disappointment over Felicity, I long for my bedroom at home. I can't help wishing for the sound of my mother's voice talking to my father and my father's deep voice replying. One of the happiest things about childhood, I have to realise now, was being upstairs in a warm bed, on the edge of sleep, and able to hear these two voices, like the voices of doves, comfortably talking to and fro, one to the other, to and fro, wonderfully peaceful and safe.

As little phrases of medieval music and the starting and stopping of the singing float, with the broken fragments of gossip, up the narrow staircase the small bedroom seems colder and more inhospitable.

'How on earth did you find this *angel*, uncompromising as she is?' Boris asks during a pause.

'*She* came to *us*,' Felicity says. 'Noël found her, or is *discovered* the right word, in the hedge.'

'A hedge-ling,' Noël says. 'It was so simple. I had hardly to raise my voice. You have to agree, darlings, that there is something of the Lorelei about me, the quality of the Lorelei has never let me down.'

'That is true,' Boris says, seeming to consider, 'I was always aware that you were attractive to *sailors*. But surely this one is not *naïve*, like Jules. This one, with all her lack of, how shall I put it, *class* is much more useful, *eddicated* as she is in the problems of ill health. She is a *medico* is she not? *Indispensable* in the face of illness.'

'Jules was not at all naïve as you say,' Felicity growls. 'He took exactly what he wanted. I never in my life was confronted by such blatant cunning ways.'

'It was *interesting* however,' Noël says in a low tone. 'Jules had *something*.'

'In any event,' Boris laughs, '*he got away*.'

After what seems a long time I hear them go outside. Boris, with great noise, starts his car. I hear their voices shrill over the engine. Laughing and coughing they stumble upstairs.

'Art thou sleeping Persephone?' I pretend to be asleep when Noël pauses at my open door. 'Persephone, sleepest thou – with the sweetest dreams?'

It is when I am trying to go down the stairs, trying to avoid the creaking steps, that Felicity follows me. She catches me at the kitchen door.

'Persephone, darling! You're only partly dressed,' she says. 'I *am sorry*,' she says, 'but you must be frozen. Come back upstairs to bed. Come into bed with us.' With her large hands on my shoulders she turns me round.

'Persephone, mounting the stairs in tears?' Noël raises himself on one elbow, his shadow in the candle light grotesque on the uneven ceiling. 'We simply must look after her.'

'Come on,' Felicity says, 'you first, in the middle.'

Unable to stop shivering, I feel their nakedness on both sides of me. I feel their warmth and their ardour.

'I caught her *escaping*,' Felicity says.

'But we need her here,' Noël, his arm reaching across me, explains. 'Persephone, you must know how much we really need you. Felix and I do really need you.'

'We are *seriously* trying to live among *real* people,' Felicity says, 'the miners, the brickworks, and the bone-and-glue people and their wives and children. You can't *leave* us now. We need your ordinariness.'

'Besides all that, I am ill,' Noël says, 'ask Felix.'

'Yes, Noël is ill,' Felicity says. 'And the Felix part, he pretends I am Felix. That is *not* his illness. That is just Noël.'

'Where can I go?' I want to ask Felicity, but instead I stare at the mud and say nothing. I can hear Noël coughing in the tiny bedroom upstairs. He has the window as wide open as he can and still feels he is not getting enough air. Sometimes he has his soup at the window, leaning on the sill with a pillow, looking out as if to see some goodness coming to him from the grass or the hedges. I wish he did not have the cough. By this time we know he has TB and we know too that the cow is tubercular and will have to be taken away to be destroyed.

Noël talks all the time. He tells me about Felicity.

'Felicity,' he says, 'Felicity with the dance, with the dancing way of walking and the slim hips, the boyish hips. Does one call this boyish?' he asks. 'Felicity-Felix-Felicity,' he says, 'with the tenor voice which must be answered, must be *rewarded* with passion. Passionately rewarded. Felicity-Felix in disguise, disguised with the clothes and the manner of the perfect housewife.

'Felicity is Felix,' Noël, feverish hot, with his arms round me, insists. 'Felix, Felicity-Felix,' he says, 'you must know . . .' He reaches then to Felicity who is on the other side of me. 'The poor child is cold.' Noël seems unable to stop talking. His cough is the only thing which stops him from talking. 'Felix,' he says, 'did you know that earlier Persephone was mounting the stairs in tears. We must, both of us, warm and comfort her.'

I lie still. I feel them moving closer.

'Let's warm her,' Noël says. 'Felix means happy,' he says. He goes on to say that Felix is Latin for lucky and Felicity comes from Felix and if you are lucky then you are happy, like Felicity is happy.

'Noël,' Felicity says, 'enjoys the power of hallucination.'

'*I am indifferent in the mornings but brave in the afternoons*,' Noël says. He wants to know which parson said these words. And how can I, he wants to know, like the smell of elderberry so much when it makes him feel sick.

'Everything,' Felicity says, 'makes Noël feel sick.'

It is not hard for me to acknowledge that these two friends of mine are the kind of people my mother and father would find difficult to like. Between them they might discuss these two, but the discussion would be limited with my mother saying they were well educated and cultured and she would then express anxiety about the drains at the farm. And my father, having only one answer to a problem of this sort, would suggest prayer and the certainty of reconciliation.

My father admires Dickens and my mother has read *The Forsyte Saga* and *Lorna Doone* in English. They both like music (hymns, my father; opera, my mother). But they do not seem to me to be on the same level as my two new friends. Even Dr Metcalf and his wife, Magda, in comparison with Noël and

Felicity, seem shallow and uncultured. Even Dr Metcalf and his gentle way of lending me books . . .

In spite of Noël's illness and my mother's increasing disapproval, the strong fragrance of the elderberry excites and pleases me and makes me rush, whenever I can, to the magical company of my two friends.

'What about Mr George?' my mother says every time I set off on the bicycle. 'What about the children?' she says. 'You have some holiday, you should go to Glasgow to the children.'

But I ignore her.

Between them, as my mother says on the day of the so-called Regency tea party, the day I plant out the cornflowers, between them, these two, she says, are wrecking my career if not my life. Between them, she says, these two are taking away what I have and are not replacing it with anything. I tell her that I do not agree with her but rather I see myself as being saved, encouraged towards all that is worthwhile and beautiful. If anything I am being rescued from having to go on solidly working my way through all the drudgery of human suffering and, as Noël says, encouraging suffering to continue by temporary alleviation and by encouraging new births. He sees me, he says, ending up in obstetrics; my black bag, complete with speculum and forceps, my only companion. Noël is very persuasive. He can see me, he says, attempting to deal with medical and surgical conditions for which there are no remedies except those surviving from folk tales and legends, in the outside leaves of lettuce and in infusions of parsley, raspberry leaves and nettles. 'Mythology,' he says, 'and witchcraft.'

Before we know about the cow, Noël has obediently swallowed a whole mug of cream every morning and, for supper, has eaten a baked apple swimming in cream. Every evening the kitchen is fragrant with the baking of clove-studded apples.

'Where can I go?' I stand at the edge of the mud wanting to ask this question. Felicity wearing the little red apron over the

loose grey flannels, the long-lasting remnants from Oxford, is
singing and humming.

> One more river and that's the river of Jordan,
> One more river and that's the river to cross.

Mostly it is humming, she is not able to remember the words.
My question is one I want to ask but I am afraid of the
answer. Small things, like the uneasy humming and singing
and an increased use of quotation in the conversation, make
me feel that they want to be rid of me. At the same time
they wait eagerly for any provisions I bring from the shops
and, whenever I arrive with a baked custard, they eat it straight
from the enamel dish in which it has been made, knocking
each other's spoons and shamelessly scraping it all up. It does
not seem to occur to them that my mother has me in mind
when she makes the custards.

Behind me Felicity is rearranging the jars of jam and bottled
fruit along the kitchen shelf. One lot, the strawberry jam, the
best-looking of them all, has been ruined. The long-handled
wooden spoon has been used for stirring some pale-blue
distemper, an improvement for the kitchen walls slapped on by
them both in turn. The tainted jam is uneatable.

> hum de hum de ha . . . that's the river to cross
> One more river and that's the river of Jordan,
> One more river and that's the river to cross.

Felicity hums and sings the few words over and over as she
moves the jars restlessly. The two of them, Noël and Felicity,
these two, have started recently to talk about me in the third
person.

It's as though we're *married* to her, Noël starts off. There's
consummation, he says. More than once, Felicity agrees. But,
Noël says, the marriage has never been *solemnized*. God, Felicity
says, that is a word I would *never* use. Ah, but the mother

81

might, Noël pretends to shake a warning finger. *Her* mother you mean, Felicity corrects Noël. *The* mother, Noël persists in a drawling voice, *the* mother, don't you agree, would approve of a solemnization. A solemnization would be precious for the mother. She would then be able to discuss the *wedding* with her friend Mrs Pudge and Mrs Pudge . . . *Pugh*, Darling, Felicity interrupts. And Mrs Pudge, Noël persists, would make suitable dresses; Noël starts to laugh, for us all, he coughs and laughs.

The idea amuses them and they go on with the joke. A wedding, they say, with invitations and table napkins to match the candles and the icing on the cake. And presents, they say, do not forget the wedding presents, we can make lists to send to guests in advance. A coffee table, Noël says; an alarm clock, Felicity says; the jug and glasses, Noël says; the table mats, his voice gains strength; matching towels, *his* and *hers*, *theirs* and *hers* . . . An oven mitt, Felicity says, another jug with glasses . . .

'We are the primary audience,' Noël says, 'for our authorship, we are the after-glow of our legend.'

'Correction,' Felicity says, '*she* is the primary etc. whatsit, primary thingamajig – audience and *she* is the after whatever it is etc.'

'You must write to the hospital,' my mother says, when I am sitting in her kitchen, 'and you must write to the children and to Miss George.'

I notice with some irritation that my mother is not able to say the names, 'Mr George' and 'Miss George', without a certain self-conscious tone and emphasis. When she says 'Mr George' it is as though she is opening his bedroom door and is, without entering the room or even looking round the door, sliding a cup of tea across the floor boards towards him.

'And another thing,' my mother says, 'your father has given away his winter coat again.'

'YOUR FATHER DON'T EVER USE THE MOSELEY ROAD'

'Your father will be home directly,' my mother says, glancing at the three-shilling alarm clock on the mantelpiece.

'You must write to the hospital,' my mother says. I am sitting in the kitchen. She glances from the noisy clock to the window as if she has heard my father open the gate. 'You must write to Miss George and to the children,' she says.

'Yes, yes,' I say and I tell her that there is no need to write to the hospital. Everything is known there. It is hard not to be irritable, but I am quiet in front of Mrs Pugh.

'To your professor then.' My mother is cutting bread and butter for my father's tea. 'You must keep in touch with him.'

'Yo'll need some things to take to that TB farm,' Mrs Pugh, who does not mince her words, as she so often tells us, says. 'I'm not one to mince my words, yo'll need *things* to last a fair while. It'll not be a weekend visit, nor a week, nor a month.'

Mrs Pugh does her treadle-machining at home and brings her hand-sewing round to my mother's kitchen. Mrs Pugh is making three nightdresses and a pink flannelette bed-jacket for me to take to the sanatorium. She wants to stitch some lace, a neat and pretty trimming, she says, on the bed-jacket. I can see it will not take her nimble fingers long.

There is a moist patch, a shadow, I have been told, on one lung. I am to be admitted to the City Sanatorium as soon as there is a vacancy for me.

In the following few days Mrs Pugh sews a blue bed-jacket for me. She, first of all, goes shopping with my mother for the right kind of material. She hems two face flannels; 'One in the wash,' she says, 'and one to use.' She makes a green bed-jacket and soon after it is finished I receive a card telling me to come the next day for admission at one o'clock.

'A couple of years,' Mrs Pugh consoles my mother. 'A couple of years and she'll be back,' she says. And she measures me for a dressing gown against the day I'll be allowed up, out of bed, to walk on the terraces in the lovely fresh air coming straight off real country fields.

'I'll allow a inch or two here and there,' she says, 'against you putting on some weight.' Mrs Pugh tells my mother that they should shop for material together unless my mother happens to have a piece of stuff by her or something which she, Mrs Pugh, could make over. 'She'll need it warm,' she says.

On the day when I'm supposed to go to the Annexe of the City Sanatorium my mother asks Mrs Pugh if she can spare the time to accompany us and Mrs Pugh, looking as she would say, affronted, as if it had never occurred to her not to come, says, 'A course! A course I'm a coming.' She points out that visiting days are the first two Sundays every month and that she can't see anything in her life to prevent her coming with my mother to visit on those days. 'They've give us the train times too,' she says.

Mrs Pugh goes on to tell us that two of her brothers were in the Annexe one time and that they are now in Australia, where they are doing all right for themselves. She says that Australia, or New South Wales as she calls it (anything with Wales in it is bound to be all right), seems to be the right idea for a great many people nowadays.

'I've always been a one to have the habit of looking ahead,'

Mrs Pugh says. 'How about if I make a flannel underlining for Mr Wright's raincoat seeing as how he's give away his top coat?'

Mrs Pugh's tea being too hot, and looking ahead to the time for leaving for the bus, she cools it in the saucer and drinks from that. A custom which, because it is Mrs Pugh's, is considered by my mother to be quite ladylike and acceptable, though she never tries it herself.

'Your father don't ever use the Moseley Road now.' My mother adopts Mrs Pugh's phrasing in her letters, in spite of the care with which she has always spoken English. Her Viennese intonation, the musical up and down of her speech, is influenced too by the high-pitched tuning, as of indignation, from the Welsh in Mrs Pugh's voice. 'He don't never want to pass the farm ever again,' my mother writes. She writes that Miss George is bringing the children down from Glasgow for a visit, but that it is not considered wise to bring them out to see me.

> *He comes home by Mount Pleasant now and the Lane even if it is longer that way and it makes him later home. It's so as not to pass the farm he comes the longer way. Do you want, do you want to have your Daddy come? Even though he's nervous about hospitals he will come if you want. He could come to see you the Sunday, as I'll have the children if you like him to come. Let us know what you want when you write. Mrs Pugh and I are coming Sunday 1st.*

During the next few days I have the feeling of homelessness which I know already, only too well. I actually look forward to visitors' day which will bring only my mother and Mrs Pugh, both of whom, after the first few minutes, when I unwrap something made by Mrs Pugh, will be dreadfully boring.

It is Mr George I want to see. Every day I hope that he will come.

'It would be nice if you could learn something useful,' my mother says. It is as if she is suggesting that, like a prisoner, I should learn a trade while I am locked up. It is the first visiting Sunday of the month.

'But I already have,' I say, stupidly near tears. 'I have, I studied. I'm a doctor, I mean . . . what else?'

'Yes, yes,' my mother says, and she hurriedly says she did not mean to upset me. 'I mean something extra that you could do while you are getting better.' She and Mrs Pugh are sitting on the wooden chairs close up to my white counterpane which the nurses call a bed mat. These bed mats are removed at night and folded up. The long ward, which is a hut really, is curved and open along one side. It is quite cheerful at night with the red blankets.

'I mean,' my mother says, still in the same reverent whisper, 'if you could learn to sew, like Mrs Pugh, that would be nice.'

The cough seems to start from somewhere out of reach and it continues persisting, irrepressible, until I have to spit and cough again and yet again, and later I lie back exhausted, flat in the flat bed, in the long flat hut in a place perhaps flatter than I have ever known a place to be. From my bed I look out over a flat view, flat to the grey horizon where some dejected horses stand, all facing the same way. Mrs Pugh says it's because of the weather the horses stand like that. It's a riding school she explains for the mentally defective, a failed horse stud, a knacker's yard. It was the same when her brothers were here, she says. The same. Even the horse riding for the idiots.

While my mother and Mrs Pugh let their attention wander, restfully watching other patients and their visitors or, with small discreet movements, sort through their own shopping bags, I too go off in my thoughts to Gertrude's Place. I have the extra-ordinary feeling that I could walk out of this ground-level ward and find, directly outside, the path through the deep grass and the cow parsley, which would bring me to the back door where

Gertrude sits plucking fowls, singeing feathers and burning quills with the little flame she nurtures in an old sardine tin beside her chair . . .

'It's not possible to go back in your life,' my mother says, as if I have said Gertrude's name aloud. 'Let me see,' she says, 'it must be twelve years since Gertrude died.'

My mother listens while I tell her that I feel well enough to walk to Gertrude's Place. She reminds me again that it is at least twelve years. I try to explain that I am getting better, knowing that all the patients share this optimism. It is part of the illness. I want to tell her that the next cough will be the one to clear away, once and for all, the debris. I stop talking and try not to cough.

With an indescribable terror I picture the haemorrhage which will, if it does not kill me, rid me of the diseased areas in my lungs and allow the quiet unseen healing to commence. I do not try to describe this to my mother.

I put myself down for needlework classes and, on the first day when I am allowed to get up, I go along to the sewing room. It is a place of gossip. The women there are mostly nurses who have been ill and are now considered to be cured. I am given unpicking to do, a nurse's uniform dress, faded and soft with washing and about to be made over as a fourth or spare uniform for someone. Fourth dresses are like this. The feeling of the worn cloth makes me remember my own fourth dresses, years ago when I was a different person. I cry a bit and understand that, though I am older and more experienced in all sorts of ways, I am no different.

I long for Mr George to come. I wait for a letter from him. He writes that he will come. He will put up at the Holly Bush and will visit me.

I am afraid that I won't get better. People don't really get better from this illness. No wonder my mother wanted me to avoid the places where there were signs. And though I want to see Mr George I feel too tired to write a letter back to him. I have an apathetic tiredness and forgetfulness and a waiting for food and not wanting the food and not wanting to talk either to the nurses or to the other patients, I do not like any of them though I know really that they are all nice people.

For some reason the River Jordan song goes round and round in my head. And though I remember all too well Felicity humming and singing on that day as she moved, without purpose, the jars of jam and bottled fruit, I go back in my mind, to school and to being in the school sanatorium with a girl called Yvonne. We sing over and over again:

> The animals came in two by two
> The elephant and the kangaroo
> One more river and that's the river of Jordan
> One more river and that's the river to cross.

I sing one line and this Yvonne girl sings the next line. In isolation (the top floor), we are by ourselves with an eye infection and not allowed to read. All our books have been removed. We sing and invent games and lean out of the window calling out to anyone who passes below. I am interested in the creamy pink and white soft flesh which is this Yvonne. It seems to me then that she is made of better material than I am made of. It is as if she is the result of generations of good breeding, not just in manners but in the making of her body, as if years and years of very good food and comfortable warm luxurious rooms have produced her. I try not to stare at her when she washes herself in a china basin the nurse sets out on the floor. Another thing is that Yvonne scarcely seems to notice my body when it is time for me to wash. In my mind I compare what I imagine her mother and father to be like with my own mother and father. Both of mine, at different times, have suffered from poverty. Yvonne and I exchange addresses, we each have a little address book. And, though we are not meant to write either, we scribble in each other's holiday address. Yvonne's address surprises me because it is with a Miss Playfair not with a Mr and Mrs, not with a father and a mother. The surname is not even the same as Yvonne's. This gives me considerable pondering which is almost as good as reading for the evening.

Not being allowed to go to the bathroom we have to sit on china pots. It is then I see the creamy hugeness of Yvonne with admiration which is tinged by my own terrible embarrassment at having to squat on the pot in the presence of someone else.

'And who does this Mr George think he is, just who does he think he is,' my mother visiting is not able to keep her voice soft. 'And worse,' she says, close up beside my bed, Mrs Pugh is not with her this time. 'Just who do you think you are, a film star or what?' She has brought a cake and a bag with chocolates and some flowers. I hardly notice the flowers and am not able to say later which, out of all the flowers, are from my visitor. I feel it is disloyal of me not to know whether my mother brought lupins or roses. And what is worse I have lost my way in the seasons. I have no idea what people in the outside world are thinking or doing or wearing. My mother always wears the same coat. Perhaps she hangs it up in the shed when she gets home. What time of the year is it?

'How can you Vera? How can you put the children out of your mind as you have done? You could at least write them half a page to thank them for their drawings . . .' My mother's voice remains close in my head after she has gone. I can hear the tears in her voice as if she is still beside me. 'And what good have they, these so-called friends of yours, done? What good has it done you, them calling you a poet and taking everything from you? You can't say I didn't warn you Vera. If I said, Vera, that they would take all you had and not replace it, they have given you *something* and it's not very nice, is it. That's why you are here in this awful place. Your Daddy doesn't sleep thinking of you in here, not getting on in your own life as you should be.'

Be fair, I want to tell my mother after she has gone to the train. Be fair, this spot on my lung could have come when I

91

was nursing high up on the balconies of the fifth floor, where the air was supposed to be fresher and cleaner and where fresh eggs, cream and nourishing soups appeared every day, sent up from those subterranean kitchens where I had once worked, hiding my first pregnancy. I want to run after my mother to tell her it was not from *them* or from my work that I have the moist patch, it could be just as easily an infection picked up during one of the long damp journeys on the bus or the train.

I want to tell her too that I *want* my children, I want to hold them and feel their soft smooth skin and to hear their voices. I did not even try to tell her that the hardest thing is being away from them, that I want to be there at their bathing and to see them wake up in the mornings.

It is true, I want to tell her, that I did not listen to her, that I was drawn in by Noël and Felicity, that they were, as she would say, making use of me, that they needed *someone*. And how could I tell her about these friends, that they called me 'poet' and that we were lovers. How would my mother understand this without being hurt by it. I think of my mother's solitary journey. She would not be able to say all she knows and thinks even if Mrs Pugh had come this time. The nurses call me doctor and tell me to come up out of the pillow. The nurses disturb me as they come round, as they always do, after visitors, with two big black metal trays. They collect all the chocolates, the biscuits, the sweets and the fruit so that the patients who do not have visitors can have a share of what is brought in.

'You must write to your professor at the hospital,' my mother says as she is leaving. Of course I must. He has written me a kind letter. I have no energy and no wish to write a reply. Another letter from Mr George lies unopened on my locker. Elke, or the other young woman, will be at Miss George's side while she, Miss George, carves the meat. Elke! How could I have allowed Elke, or anyone, to take my place in that household. Elke, drying my children after their baths. Elke, sitting up there on my cherry-wood floor.

Felicity and Noël. I want to know where they are and if they

know where I am. *Felicity, I wonder, will you come to see me.*
Felicity and Noël please please come to visit me . . .

Sometimes, like now, my thoughts are too heavy. While I
was studying I thought that when I qualified everything would
be different, that I would be raised in some way because of
passing my exams and because of being able to understand the
work I would be doing and in the knowing more about human
life. And I thought I would be wiser myself and on the same
level as other people instead of the wrong level. But it is not
like this. I make the same mistakes. I want the same things I
have always wanted and always I am on the edge of other people.
Patients and illness are on one side of life and romantic beauty
and ideals seem to be removed to another unreachable side. And
then there are the obligations, the special obligations special
people have towards each other. If I am to be outside or only
a part of a special obligation it is not enough.

I want to be the giver and the recipient of the whole and it
seems that I never shall be.

The cough when it comes seems to start somewhere out of reach,
it is a small cough and persistent. If someone else had the cough
within my hearing I would be intolerant. It is my way of
coughing, as if I am not coughing, which would irritate me if
someone else was the one coughing.

The sputum mugs, all shabby and chipped, make me feel sick,
they are ugly in the way they are made and ugly in their reason
for being there. I know that there are all kinds of sputum and that
the nurses are trained to observe the amount, the colour, the
odour, the tenacity – whether it clings to a patient's lips or is
difficult to spit out. I am shy of this being watched. I know that
they want to know whether it is coughed up early in the
mornings or after a meal or after any kind of exertion. I know all
the descriptions of sputum; *abundant or scanty, clear or opaque,
muco-purulent, bloodstained or rusty*. It might be *frothy*, it
might look like *the juice of prunes* or *like egg yolk* or, in my

diagnosis, *like sago grains. It can come up, if it does come up, in coin-shaped masses lying on the bottom of the vessel into which it is expectorated. This occurs when cavities are present.*

The ordinary sputum cup has a little antiseptic placed at the bottom for the sputum to fall on. Patients who are allowed up have a pocket sputum flask made of blue glass with a screw-top lid and this, in order to avoid soiling the pocket, should be provided with a separate removable calico pocket . . .

For disposal, sputum may be poured over sawdust which is afterwards burnt.

It is all too familiar for me, this ugliness of the illness. This ugliness belonged earlier to other people and now it seems to be my possession.

Whenever I can, when I am allowed out of my bed, I leave the sputum mug in the most out-of-the-way places. There are not many such places.

'Where is your sputum mug?'

'I don't have any sputum.'

Hides sputum, is recorded along with my temperature, pulse and respiration.

There is no music here, only the sound of coughing. Endless coughing of the hopeless sort.

At first I do not understand that I am wishing for music. When my mother comes I almost tell her about the music, that I am missing it. She tells me she has brought me something to read. She has brought, she says, *Lorna Doone* and *The Forsyte Saga*.

'But I read these at school.'

'Never mind! You can read them again.' My mother goes on to say that she enjoyed them more the second and even the third time round.

That night, when Noël and Felicity have gone to bed, that night after their talk about a wedding, as if they want to hurt me

94

by their talk, I am not able to sleep. I go downstairs and out into the field and see the moon. I have forgotten about the moon. My father always said that he thought of the moon as his moon. When I looked at the moon, he always told me, I was seeing the same moon as he was seeing, however far apart we might be. Just now in this place I am not all that far away from where my father is. It seems to be a great distance because we are not able to speak of the things which would make a bridge across that space between my earth and his moon.

I look up at the moon and set off walking across the field in the dark. When I reach the hedge and the road, I follow the road not choosing any special direction. Simply I am walking away from Noël and Felicity, these two, who are my friends.

The familiar fragrance of elderberry and the steady muffled snoring of a city, apparently asleep but awake with nocturnal industry remind of the carelessness of childhood and enhance the reality of what it feels like to have no place to go home to.

My mother no longer walks this road, the Moseley Road, with me. There is no fluting voice with gentle warnings about spots of blood in the snow and no wise consolations for a girl crying in the black shadow of the elderberry. No *other* girl, I should say because I am the one now, the one crying here at the side of the empty road wanting my mother.

On the day when the doctor comes to see Noël the towels and sheets are dismal, hanging grey and low, almost dragging across the mud. I watch the doctor, through the mist, as he leaves his car and picks his way across the wet field. He is a small man in a suit which has a waistcoat. A looped and golden watch-chain shines on the worsted cloth. His spats are the colour of field mushrooms. His shoes are well polished. He carries a small case and, with a light step, crosses the mud, balancing on the plank and goes straight into the house without knocking.

'Which one? Which one are you with?' the doctor asks me on his way out. He glances, as he speaks, to the upstairs window which is now hanging by one hinge, Noël having wrenched it out of the frame in his desperation for more air.

'Which one?' the doctor asks again, jerking his head in the direction of the wrecked window. I look down at the mud. Immediately he apologizes. He says he is sorry, he begs my pardon in an old-fashioned sort of way. I imagine him begging pardon before the performance of an internal examination. It would be a performance. He puts his case down on the doorstep and scribbles quickly on a small pad. Tearing off the page, he hands it to me and tells me to report to the City Clinic for a chest X-ray.

He crosses the mud and stops on the first tuft of grass. 'Is there any way,' he says, 'is there any way that you can get away from here?' he asks. 'It's not a place at all to live in. No place at all. It's filthy and there's no drainage.' He moves on then, as if dancing and balancing on the drier bits of ground. As he goes, I hear him muttering, 'And wherever is the drinking water coming from?'

I notice every detail about the doctor because he seems to represent all the safety and cleanliness in my mother's house when I was small. He reminds me of the doctor who came, his hands warm and sweet with the scent of carbolic, to my bedside once, with one of my mother's best teaspoons in a clean napkin, to examine my throat when I had measles. I want to run after Noël's doctor. I want to tell him I can't stand the dirt any longer. I begin to cry, I can't stop the tears running down my face.

There is no sound from the upstairs bedroom. No coughing and no complaining. And then I hear Felicity coming downstairs.

'*You must take another road*,' Felicity appears in the doorway. She leans on the door post. Her handsome face is more careworn than usual and seems thinner and deeply lined especially round the mouth. '*You must take another road*,' she goes on, '*if you wish to escape from this wild place*. I am paraphrasing Dante,' she says, 'Canto 1, page 9'. Felicity yawns, as if bored in advance on seeing me. The pale sun offers no warmth. The wet washing hangs motionless. Though the mist is dispersing the cold rises through my shoes.

Felicity yawns in a well-bred way into the mist.

Felicity sees them before I do. She sees the two people, in dark coats, pausing in the narrow space between the elderberry and the hawthorn. She sees them pausing and peering across the field. Then I see my mother's white hat and my father's white face.

'They must have come on the bus and walked from the corner,' I say. I want to run over the wet grass to the opening in the hedge. I want to go over to them, but I stay as if nailed to the rough wood of the kitchen window sill. I do not look a second time across to where they are.

Unperturbed, Felicity comments in a low voice about the ludicrous, the unforgettable and *ludicrous*, a white hat with an old bottle-green winter coat. She continues her recitation;

'*Wherefore I think I discern this for thy best that thou follow me; and I will be thy guide and lead thee hence through an eternal place . . .*'

I look up quickly as Felicity speaks and yawns, for a moment I think she is asking me to go away with her. I love and admire Felicity. Her face has no smile, only the tired sad look.

'All you have to do Persephone, *Darling*,' she says, 'is to substitute "them" for "me" and "they" for "I". Dante, *Darling*, same page probably. In an English translation naturally. You should go with your illustrious and suffering ma and pa.' And then in a voice suddenly harsh, she says that an ambulance is coming for Noël. I want to comfort Felicity, I want to tell her that I know how weak and ill Noël is. I want to tell her too that it will be better for him to be properly looked after. Felicity jerks her head in the direction of the cow saying that something, whatever it is they use for animals, will come for her. 'Do they have animal ambulances?' she asks. When I look at the cow I feel ashamed that I have never paid attention to her condition.

I have never noticed how sharply her bones show all over her emaciated body.

Felicity is not allowed to travel in the ambulance with Noël. We watch as Noël is carried, grey faced with his eyes closed, to the ambulance. He opens his eyes and turns his head and says, with his handsome smile, '*Exit, pursued by a bear. Enter the Shepherd. Shakespeare.*' And closes his eyes.

Felicity takes all the money I have and races off across the field to be in time for the next bus.

I wait all day for Felicity to come back. I scrub some potatoes and bake them in the kitchen fire to have something hot for her. I wait all evening for her to come home. Several times I go out to look into the darkness, wanting to hear her voice calling across the field. I listen to the rats scrabbling in the walls of the kitchen. Felicity does not come. I gather as many things as I can push into one of the old hessian sacks used for potatoes and cabbages and I set off for the road. Once there, it is easier to walk and I drag the sack. Because of the great size of the enormous pit mound it seems to be moving alongside, keeping up with me, an ugly black hump, a deformity hiding the moon for a long time.

My father opens the door. He has opened the door so often for me during my life that it seems to be quite natural for him to open it in the middle of the night. He has pulled on his trousers, his night shirt is only partly tucked in. My mother is half way down the stairs which come down to the hall immediately inside the front door. She is pulling her coat on over her night dress.

My father, with all the years of good manners stored up inside him, takes the sack gently as if it had the same quality about it as a fashionable leather suitcase complete with straps and keys and labels.

'Put the kettle on,' he tells my mother, 'and give the fire a good rake, it'll soon come up.'

My mother cries a bit at the kitchen table, while my father rattles about in the coal place for suitable small bits to bring up the fire.

'You'd like a nice bath,' he says to me. It is then that I remember almost the last thing Noël said the day before. He said that he was going to emulate Socrates by having his ultimate bath early so that neither of us, Felicity or I, would have the trouble of washing him after he was dead.

Because of her opinion of Mrs Pugh, my mother understanding that Mrs Pugh *knows*, agrees that Australia has great possibilities. Though for me any possibility of this sort is too far away for any consideration. The future is something vague and unattainable since something frightening and impossible has presented itself and there is no way round it.

THE WIDOW AND
THE MIGRANT

'Tell me about yourself, Migrant,' the rice-farm widow says to me. So I tell my widow things about myself. When I tell her about Felicity and Noël her mouth is so wide open, as she listens, I can see her gold fillings. At that time, I think her whole fortune is in her mouth.

'You mean to tell me!' she says. 'Oh, I can't believe . . .' she says, 'that they, I mean, *together*. You can't mean *that*.'

'Yes, that's right,' I tell her.

'Oh, Migrant. You poor child, poor poor child.'

'Oh no, your widowship, not at all. Nothing like that. They were very gentle and considerate. They were intellectuals, don't you see. The whole thing was more of an *idea*. And it was quite a joke thing between us, between the three of us, every time. Their very good manners, don't you know.'

'More than once! Heavens, child!'

'Please, please – don't be concerned. Do not concern your gracious self; it was funny, really funny. They were, *unlike us*, so very polite.'

'You mean, "*after you*" and "Oh no, *after you*".'

'Well sort of, not quite, but yes, rather like that.'

'What an *experience* you had.'

'I suppose so.'

"You *suppose* so. My dear Migrant, do you realise that plenty of people would give their eye teeth . . .'

'But what would anyone *do* with someone else's eye teeth?'

We use these special names for each other, Widow and Migrant. Straight away, before the ship begins to roll, we use them, at the table, on the deck, in the bar and during conversations, which Mr George says, contain the language of the prelude to our, hers and mine, curious flirtation.

Widow and Migrant, sometimes adding 'the', the Widow and the Migrant, so that we distance ourselves into a third-person narration. Particularly we do this during our daily shopping in the ship's shop, choosing expensive unnecessary clothing, gifts and perfume.

'Would the Widow like this?'

'The Migrant ought to have one of these. No, I tell a lie, the Migrant should have two. Make that half a dozen.' The widow opens her sequined purse and keeps it open dangling over one arm.

I have to admit, privately to myself, that I am surprised straight away at this distinction I possess in my ability to be someone quite different if an occasion demands a difference, the putting forward of a changed self. I reflect on this change, this ability, every time I have a shower in the widow's own bathroom. I have to understand that I was conscious of the need for a change in my demeanour as soon as I boarded the ship. If I pause and look back I can see that I have been capable of putting on this sort of armour, this shell, a kind of protection, at various times during my life. I have to understand too that if I do not like this quality in myself, Mr George, as well, might dislike it.

As the weather becomes warmer, I fret for my one pair of shorts packed without foresight, unreachable in the hold. At the appropriate time the ship's shop overflows with a summer display.

'You'd best have some of these,' the widow says, making a

competent selection. 'Australian shorts are properly cut and tailored. You can't possibly *be seen* in English shorts.'

Meanwhile, Mr George, who is nearby in a long chair reading about the *unexplainable glow of legend* and *how a man cannot hope to live longer than the ultimate worth of his possessions*, glances across with, what is to me, an unfamiliar sort of smile. Neither of us have ever met anyone like the widow before. Mr George's new way of smiling and his public devotion to reading are, in part, a little mask to hide his uneasiness about his new appointment and this long journey towards it. I know this, for my own thoughts insist on leaping forward to possible strangeness and difficulties in my work and, at the same time, I am worrying whether Helena, when she starts the term at her boarding school, will be happy. And I wonder if Miss George is managing well enough with Rachel. Elke, the au pair with a triumphant and fearless laugh, seems very suitable. I try to hope that the children are happy and I rest in this hope.

Straight away after meeting the rice-farm widow I think it strange that there should be, all at once, another widow in my life making now a total of four if I count Gertrude and Magda, though it is never clear if Dr Metcalf died on active service as a result of an accident or whether he is somewhere alive still and living with Smithers, the poetry-writing Theatre Orderly with whom Dr Metcalf was in love and, it was said, went to the front when the war was practically over, in reality, in pursuit of Smithers. If, after all this time, Dr Metcalf is still alive Magda cannot, even though she is alone, be classed as a widow. And the fourth widow, the railway-man's widow with her pronouncements and her ability with the sewing machine, being as it were the chosen property of my mother, does, like the others, slip out of my mind in the presence of this new and even more powerful widow.

'I always take two napkins,' the widow says, 'one for the mouth and one for the lap.' After a pause during which we are fully occupied with cold cuts on rye, new and unfamiliar for me, innovative I want to say but, because of the heavy grain, the word sticks, the widow says, 'And what about your gentleman?' She untangles a bit of beef from what she calls her partial, her *unsatisfactory* partial.

'Oh please, *not* gentleman,' I manage in a scattering of cress.

'Well, Migrant, your professor then. How does he respond to Beethoven, I mean not just the last five quartets, let's say the first and second symphonies?' The widow signals the steward and asks for coffee. 'I mean,' she continues, 'they are a downright statement of passion which cannot be denied. And then again what about the drums in Beethoven's seventh?' While my widow talks I think of the time when my mother took me to a concert and, because of worrying about the people who might be late and not allowed in till the interval, I did not hear the music at first. I remember now the way in which the drummer hurled himself into the music. At the time it is a revelation.

'Body and soul,' my widow is still talking about the seventh symphony, 'and exercising great restraint at the same time.' She has come to the drummer now and is talking about restraint. 'Has your gentleman, your professor, the power of restraint?' I almost tell my widow about my mother, that she is no longer the same as she was, now that she has her own widow, Mrs Pugh.

'Has he, your professor, ever mentioned a response to the symphonies?' she asks. Mr George joins us at the small table. He, from being on the deck a great deal, lying back in a long chair, reading, has a healthy suntanned look. The widow, without any hesitation about making personal remarks, says that Mr George's white hair and the suntan go well together. That the combination makes him look more distinguished than ever. She goes on to say that she would like to see him in a specially tailored, white, raw-silk jacket and that we should have one made during the voyage. There is no chance then for me to try to answer the widow's questions. She could even ask Mr George himself. She seems to be that sort of woman. She will ask anything she wants to know. Mr George acknowledges my widow's compliment with a smile. It is not the kind of smile

I want for myself from him but, at present, any look or smile would make me feel better – a look or a smile from Mr George, that is.

I often reflect on the idea of 'widow', of being a widow and, that being a widow means that you are something special, that you have been selected and publicly chosen at some time in your life. The idea of being chosen means that someone has made a sensitive choice of taste and touch and has been drawn irresistibly – even if you live alone later.

The word widow and the idea of widow suggest black clothes, a soft spreading bosom and a lap, overfed and overweight. Included in the idea of widow is shining silky material, if not black perhaps a subdued violet or the colour of a gentle petal, a mauve cyclamen perhaps. These images of widowhood do not fit exactly with my rice-farm widow. She never wears violet, and black only for funerals. Black would need something sparkling and hideously expensive, she explains, or else something fresh and tender and youthful.

The kiss the widow gives me, when we are just through the double doors leading from the deck to the top of the brass-bound stairs which go straight down to the dining rooms, is not a cool-lipped brushing of a powdered cheek crumpling against mine. It is a compelling kiss, masterful and tender at the same time, with a perfume on her breath of sophisticated exotic drinks and an overpriced suntan lotion with a foreign name.

She's been in the sun all day, she tells me then, on the top deck with nothing on except a wisp of cotton to protect her nipples. Then there was a bit of a party, she explains, and when she told the Purser that if she went on drinking she'd be under the Captain, she thought she had better leave. 'It's my Big Mouth,' she says.

'Come to my cabin,' she says, so I go.

When I was thinking about all the widows, counting them up, I included Gertrude but, in fact, she was not a widow.

'To all intents and purposes, Gertrude was not really a widow,' I say. But my widow is not listening, she is ferreting about in her cupboards, her cases and her special boxes. She has something she wants me to wear if she can find the accessories, she says.

Gertrude wasn't a widow, I am remembering exactly as my mother tells me that time when I ask her. It is as though I hear my mother's voice through the throbbing of the ship. For some time we have been plunging as well as rolling. Quite a different movement from the smooth sailing at first.

'Gertrude,' my mother explains, 'had a husband but you won't ever have seen him. He was a farm labourer,' she says, 'with ten shillings a week. He walked miles to his work before it was light in the mornings and would have been walking back by the field paths in the evenings. You would already have left Gertrude's and been on your way home.'

My mother says that they, Gertrude and her husband, did not have much to say to each other and, she says, they slept each in a shabby chair, one on either side of the hearth. It is not hard for me to imagine them both in the ragged armchairs, one on either side of the fireplace with the kettle humming softly on the hob between them. And where, every now and then, a hot cinder would dislodge and fall, with a small flare of light and warmth through the broken bars of the grate, breaking their sleep.

Gertrude, my mother says, used to declare that the cat they had for seventeen years used to prick up her ears and set off at a certain time through the grass and the weeds to meet Gertrude's husband. It did not matter which field path he had taken when setting out for the long slow walk home, the cat never failed to take the right direction and it would come back with him, treading lightly where he trod, pausing if he paused and *measured* in that the cat did not outstep him, but like his own shadow following him, she would not arrive home before he did.

It seems incredible to me, at that time, that my mother actually seems to know more about Gertrude than I do.

'You can't count Gertrude as one of the widows in your life,' my mother says. 'She died before her husband died. Everybody at some time or other knows a widow,' my mother goes on, 'and not all your friends are widows. Miss George,' she says, 'is a spinster and so is your Aunt Daisy. Neither of them can be widows.'

I think of other nurses at the hospital. I think of Trent and remember that she was a widow, proud of her black clothes, but only briefly. And I wonder about Lois and if she ever married; and then there was Ramsden. What about Ramsden?

'It does not look,' my mother says, 'as if you will ever be a widow.' She is bending over the washing-up bowl with her back to me at the time, so I do not know what her face is like when she is saying this.

'I'll have to go to the toilet or else my back teeth'll be under water,' my widow, with an armful of clothes, beads and chains dangling from her fingers, comes up from a final box interrupting my unexpected memories.

'Put this on,' she says to me, 'with this head band and the beads, lots and lots of beads,' she says, 'and you'll love the fringe when it settles round your legs. See what I mean?'

It was like having to listen to music alone, the rice-farm widow tells me, or reading something and having no one to talk to about what you've read. 'It's not having anyone to tell things to,' she says. 'Wealth and prosperity,' she goes on while I watch her pulling out more clothes. She's changing for dinner. 'Wealth and prosperity are nothing unless you have someone to enjoy them with.' She was not, she says then, one of the usual fat overdressed women, obliged to travel round the world using up the money their husbands had made, working themselves to an early death in the process.

'I did all the work myself,' she says.

She has thighs as straight and as muscular as an athlete half her age might have. She makes me stand, she invites me, I should say, to stand barefoot on her stomach. She asks if I can feel her muscles and I tell her yes I can.

I thought, I tell my widow, that it would be so wonderful to be with Mr George day and night, day after day and night after night during the voyage. I tell her that is not how we have been able to travel, to arrange our travelling, I explain. His university has arranged his ticket and my hospital has arranged mine. When I say ticket I mean passage, I begin further explanation but the widow interrupts.

'Officially you are not together,' she says, 'and before you left both of you thought that this would not matter. Unfortunately,' she continues, '*husband* and *wife* stupidly do matter even on board ship unless you are the bold type and neither of you is bold and,' the widow says, 'scandal in Acadeem is greatly enjoyed. I can just imagine,' she says, 'the university wives in their hats and gloves at their tea club whispering . . .'

'He travelled, my deah, with a woman who is not his wife . . .'

'Who on earth is she?

'She's supposed to be a doctor if you please . . .

'She's got children, I've heard she has children . . .

'Yes, she's left her children, would you believe *with his sister*!'
My widow changes from her sixth-form schoolgirl voice to one of immediate understanding and sympathy saying that, during the war, people made allowances, boy friends going overseas, that sort of thing. But that now, twelve or thirteen years later, propriety has returned, decorum and the pleasure, during plain and dull times, of gossip.

'Does he,' she asks suddenly, 'does your gentleman professor admit to paternity?'

Her question surprises me. 'It would only be for one,' I tell my widow, trying not to show that her question has been a shock. 'It was such a short time,' I tell her. 'I could, for all they knew, have been pregnant when they took us in. Helena was four. D'you see, they, Mr George and Miss Eleanor, they never asked me anything. Later I told Mr George every single thing about my life.'

I tell my widow then about the snow I shovelled off the flat roof, about the Beethoven quartet by Mr George's study fire in the evening, and about Mr George liking my red cheeks, red because of the cold earlier when I was on the roof.

I tell her about Mr George's narrow iron bed and the tears trembling along Miss George's eyelashes the next morning when I take her little round tea tray into her room and she is lying there as if asleep still, only I know she is not asleep because she is crying.

'There never has been,' I say, 'a time which was the right time for telling her. But Mr George, he knows.'

'If you ask me,' my widow says, 'she, Miss George, she knows it too.'

After a bit she asks me how old I am. I tell her that I'm thirty-four. She says do I realise that at thirty-four or -five a woman has reached her sexual plateau. She is, at thirty-five, at her highest level of sexuality and therefore at her most desirable.

On the way down to dinner the widow says to me to come to the bar first.

'Migrant,' she says, 'I'll shout you.' I'm not sure what she means but I go with her all the same.

The ship is a so-called one-class ship for the purposes of the voyage. Some passengers like Mr George and my widow have very spacious and comfortable cabins and people like me share, usually four people to one cabin.

The widow, my widow, should have had a fellow passenger

but she must have missed the ship. The widow rejoices. She has her own bathroom.

'Feel free, Migrant,' she says, tossing a thick first-class type bath towel to me. I do not mind at all going with her to her cabin and I am very glad to use her luxurious bathroom as the three young women, with whom I share, seem to spend all their time locked in the bathroom doing things to their immature legs or to their complicated hair.

'Thank you, Widow. Much obliged, your Widowship,' I say adopting a tone of voice which causes her to laugh. I like to make her laugh.

The widow is used to the word widow. She uses it all the time and mixes a great deal, if scornfully, with other widows. As she says herself, there is no escaping them or migrants on board ships like the one we are travelling on. I never thought of myself as a migrant but that is what I am. A migrant, if only temporarily, my appointment like Mr George's being for one year with possibilities of extension. Mr George's is more in the nature of an invitation.

I tell my widow that it is because of Mr George and Miss George that I have been able to study and to qualify in medicine. The widow bets all the same that my mother and father would have turned themselves inside out to put me through and would not have required me as a maid or for *other services*. I have no reply to this.

I am still trying to get used to this migrant thing.

MIGRANTS QUEUE HERE MIGRANTS CHEST X-RAY NO MIGRANTS PAST THIS POINT MIGRANTS REPORT HERE

and so on. I am still trying to get used to all this I tell her.

'Your father,' the widow says straight away, when she sees I am crying by the rail on the top deck. 'Your father,' she pats me on the back, a thump it is really, more of a correction than a consolation, 'your father can't accompany you all the way in your life. There are definite times, are there not, when you would not want him.' She is on her way, she says, to bat the guts out of all the other widows in a deck-tennis tournament. She would have preferred, she adds over her handsome shoulder, a game of quoits, the sharp-edged, ankle-biting iron sort. I hear her low rumble of laughter, gradually disappearing, all the way to the other end of the ship.

Often during the voyage I feel a curious sense of isolation in spite of all the people on the ship, and in spite of the presence, if at a distance, of Mr George. And even the widow seems removed when the emptiness settles like a mist all round me. The ship, a substantial and portly sea-going duchess, seems to plough bravely on an unknown course. When I try to speak of this to Mr George, when we meet at the rail, he laughs and says that ships are making this journey all the time and that I feel as I do feel because we are making the voyage for the first time. There is nothing in the sea to show us the way, I tell him and he laughs again and says have I forgotten who was the mentor on another first-time occasion.

'How barren Crete looks,' I say to the widow when all the passengers are pushing to be at the rail to photograph a thin distant line of land which has appeared as if from nowhere. 'Just a few flat houses and some skinny trees and scrub. The people there must be very poor and ignorant.'

'I'll bet,' she says then, 'they know a thing or two we don't know.' She says to wait till we get to the Great Bitter Lake, Port Said and Suez. 'But this sea,' she says, 'I had it from your gentleman, your professor, this morning, this sea is the special sea where Odysseus swam for nine days, nine days on end, mind you! There's a thought.'

The ship at anchor, rolling slightly waiting for passage through the Suez Canal, seems as if suspended and lost. Bereaved, as if without hope of reaching a destination. When I stand at the ship's rail, up on the top deck, the expanse of water, disappearing into a sky of the same colourless opaque quality, seems to provide a visual but silent response to my loneliness. This quality

111

matches the sound of the Arabic music heard faintly in Mr George's cabin during the day and the night. It is a thin wailing song from within the raised panelling or, if imagined as being from the fringes of the land, it is a solitary note, sustained on a single breath, crying in the reeds. It is a sound refined and filtered from one remote culture to another through the mixture of materials, the steel and the brass, the timber, the glass and the fumed oak in the massive structure which is the ship.

A ship is a closed unnatural world in which it is not possible for us to live as we would like to live, Mr George tells me during the time I am with him in his cabin. I never stay there all night and some nights do not go in there at all. He tells me that later we shall be together every night and go, each of us, to our work and come together every night without impediment of any sort. He tells me he is impatient for this. Taking me in his arms he says he is sure he does not have to remind me of all that exists between us during the years I have been with him and with Miss George. Gently he tells me how much I mean to him and that anything that has to do with me and my life is his concern and is more important than anything else.

'How would you like fat-head for a nickname?' This detail from a conversation, overheard, coming into my head during Mr George's tender embrace surprises me. I feel his quick little kisses on my hair, my forehead and the side of my neck as he holds me close. I try not to remember sitting with my widow, earlier, on the white-painted chairs by the swimming pool, the Tavern Bar, conveniently as my widow says, immediately behind us, both of us submerging our freshly applied lipstick, *chameleon cerise*, in the deep whipped cream of her favourite Brandy and Benedictine coffee, brought to us without it being ordered, in tall, fluted, silver-rimmed glasses.

I pull Mr George down on his bunk, pulling him close and trying to unfasten our clothes and discard them quickly.

'If anyone called *me* fat-head,' the indignant voice continues in my thoughts, in the clipped overtones of outrage and shock and the need for imitation horn-rimmed spectacles to be removed and breathed on and polished with a handkerchief, 'I would,' the voice rising goes on, 'I would certainly not be able to think of them as *friend*, would you? I mean, think of it, *fat-head*.' The reply from horn-rimmed's companion, at the time, is lost in one of the widow's long rumbling coughs during which she laughs, snorts, wipes her eyes, chokes, hiccups and throws away her slim cigar.

'How about shit-head, darlin'?' she manages at last, but politely only just loud enough for me to hear. And then she is shaking with suppressed mirth and we quiver together close on the wrought-iron and I feel a desire for her which is overpowering. She looks into my eyes with an intensity which is at once kind and loving and fierce. My eyes fill with foolish tears.

'Later,' she whispers. And then, in the accents of the fat-head shock and the imitation horn rims, she says, 'Afterwards we shall both go on a water diet, cold bathings, cold douchings and cold water to drink . . .' With an added, 'Scooze I', also horn-rimmed and a little too loud after a lengthy characteristic burring coughing fit mixed with hiccups.

'Is it your new friend?' Mr George asks a few minutes later. 'I suppose,' he says, 'it's an excitement, the new friend.'

'Look at the menu, child,' the widow says. '*Migrant! You don't want curried wings.* There's nothing on a chicken's wings. Bring two porterhouse steaks,' she says to the steward. 'Make that three,' she says as Mr George, approaching our table, pauses at the empty chair. 'Make 'em rare,' the widow continues, 'with fried potatoes and salads. Baguette or rye?' She turns to Mr George, holding out the little basket and smiling with approval. I glance at Mr George sideways. This is something I have never done before. He has not been on deck all morning and when I knocked on his cabin door only Mr Street was there making up the cabin, as he said, his breath sweet with whisky. Street is Mr George's cabin steward. The widow knows him and has warned Mr George not to give him his tip, which should be about two pounds, till disembarkation.

'Or he'll be slumped drunk inside the cabin against the door and you'll not be able to get in,' the widow says when giving this advice. Her own steward is called Smith and he had his two pounds early on with the promise of another two later. Consequently the widow gets additional services like having deep hot baths run for her and two warmed towels handed round the door when required. A woman does out the cabin I'm in and the widow says there's no need to give her anything unless I have an old jumper or a dress I can't wear any more.

'There is so much to learn about ship travelling,' I say, in order to say something after Mr George has seen my sideways look at him.

'I'll go along with that,' the widow says as our laden plates arrive. 'And people too,' she says, 'there's a lot to learn about people and a ship's a good place for learning.'

I look down at my plate and try to concentrate on the steak. Without wanting to I am remembering the night, what little remained of the night, before I left Mr George's cabin for my own. I am unable to forget Mr George's words.

'That woman, that vulgar woman, her talk about music, for one thing, is the kind of rubbish put on record sleeves to enable people like her to talk as if they enjoy music and know something about it. How can you, Vera, be so taken in by someone like this?'

I try to tell him that the widow is only trying to be friendly and that I'm not being, as he says, taken in. I try to explain that I need friends, especially on board the ship since I have left everyone, my children included. Especially my children.

I am surprised then, well amazed really, when he tells me he has spoken to Miss George by wireless telephone and that all is well at home.

'Did you speak to the children?' I ask him and he says, yes he did and they spoke to him.

So that was why I was unable to find him on deck, he must

114

have been in some office or other making this fantastic telephone call from the ship.

'The children,' I say. 'You heard their voices?' Mr George tells me yes he did hear their voices and, he said, that Helena wanted me to know that she had on a pair of my silk stockings, the honey-coloured ones from Marshalls, and that her legs, she thinks, look nice in them.

With the beating of the pulses in my head and neck drowning the thin nocturnal Arabic wailing, which is their music, imprisoned as it seems to be within the woodwork of Mr George's cabin, I do not cry until I am under the blankets in the bunk in my own cabin.

The widow is telling us that we'll both have to learn to eat meat, to really eat it. She glances at our unfinished plates and jerks her head towards the table next to ours where a clean-looking family with three children have ordered steaks. 'Even a whole T-bone for the little boy who only looks about seven,' she says.

'You'll have to learn to eat more meat,' she says once more. And then she tells me that I'll have to know how to choose it and cook it. She says she'll teach me the cuts of beef and lamb. She says no one, but no one, can live in Australia without this simple knowledge. Mr George appears to be not taking much notice of my widow's remarks. I feel responsible for his silence. I am not accustomed to being in what amounts to a social encounter with him. I wonder if other people feel this sort of responsibility. In the silence while we are cutting up and moving little amounts of food about our plates I notice the people on the other side of us. Probably two married couples, an ugly but useful phrase, which is painful for me, but which cannot be disregarded, all four are picking at salads and staring about with bored mournful expressions. They pick a bit and stare, another pick and another stare, slack mouthed with what looks like unhappiness. I seem to see these reflections of unhappiness in all kinds of places, in the narrow passages, on the decks, in the communal wash rooms where women, in passing, smile with forlorn hope at themselves forced by the mirrors to see themselves often from more than one angle. Especially too, there are reflections in the shining brass door fittings which distort heads and bodies. Engraved on the brass floor plates are familiar factory names from the Midlands in England. Why these names, familiar as they are, but without any personal connection, should make me wish to be back there visiting Noël and Felicity, or my mother and father, or going back to earlier times, visiting Gertrude, is unexplainable. In the continued silence of the meal I remember seeing the factory names from the bus or the train. These brass things are simply a part of the ship, nothing more, except that they come from the place where I come from.

I am surprisingly unhappy that Mr George is staying on at the table. Though I am not a bereaved person I have my own share of deep wounds to which I am responding in secret. I suppose, if I think about this, so is Mr George. I am surprised that I am able to suddenly think this about Mr George. Outwardly neither of us reveals anything. No one can guess, on seeing us, that something from before is still between us. Even my widow, who seems to see through everything. Though I feel afraid and perhaps relieved at the same time that, before the next landfall, she will drag the whole sad story from me.

'A real conversation stopper,' my widow says, when Mr George leaves the table with a polite little nod after, I suppose, giving up the idea of waiting for me. 'Your gentleman,' my widow goes on, 'your professor certainly is a man of few words.' I say that we should excuse Mr George because he is preparing lectures for his new appointment.

'Migrant!' the widow says, 'never ever excuse a man for anything and do not have milk in the coffee. Powdered milk, as *you* should know *ruins* everything. Plenty of sugar,' she says, 'but no milk.' She orders the steward to bring two Napoleons in warmed balloons. 'Men must make their own reasons and excuses,' she says. 'Never excuse a man,' she says again, 'a man, like an illness, can separate people, can break a friendship . . .' The widow stops talking as the tears spill stupidly down my face. I tell her that I know I'm silly. I tell her that I keep meeting myself on this ship, that I want to leave, to get off this ship. Would it be possible to get off and go back, say, from the next port? 'I must get off,' I sob, 'I want to go back to my children.' I tell my widow about Mr George having the telephone call without my knowing. My widow does not say anything. She holds her brandy beneath her appreciative nose and, ignoring my crying, advises me to do the same.

'It's like an inhalant,' she explains, 'think of it as a menthol camphor or a friar's balls.'

'Friars' Balsam, your Widowship.' I regain some sort of composure and feel ashamed.

'Yes, you're right,' my widow says. She tells me to think things out for myself, a journey is a good time for this. She says, that for many years, she seemed to have existed purely to keep accounts, to pay wages and to answer letters, to telephone the vet, the doctor, the manager, the shearing sheds, the kitchen and to prepare reports for agricultural journals and conferences *and* to order and prepare endless meals.

'Sometimes in unbearable heat,' she says, 'going over the books at night looking for the mistakes.' She was a sort of machine until one day she took it upon herself to make changes. She tells me how she learned to take short cuts during her most busy times. She only used the china which would go safely through the dishwasher. She put away her silver and her antique dishes. 'I used to put my husband's biscuits on a saucer,' she says, instead of the gold-edged special plates for cakes and biscuits. 'On a saucer,' she says, 'an old saucer just as if for a cat!' The gold-edged antique china had to be washed by hand so she stopped using it. The gold, which she loved, had been washed off some things, she says before she realised what dishwashers did. She is referring, she says, to her dinner service.

'All my gold edges are plain white now,' she says, 'but the cupboards are still crammed with good china and of course all my silver is put away in the bank. Change over from rice,' she says, 'to sheep, and change from silver to stainless steel. Easy!'

I try in the dining room, where we are the only ones left, to imagine what her house and her life are like. I almost confess that I have never seen a dishwasher and that, in any case, I would call it a washing-up machine.

You can be a widow in more than one sense, she tells me, you can be widowed from one style of life to another, from one set of household duties to another.

'I must have been one of the first with a dishwasher. You should have seen it. Huge.' She pronounces it Hooghe. 'All white enamel, took up the whole kitchen, also had hoses in the sink. Guess!' she says, 'who left the hoses out on the floor.' The enamel chipped off, 'flew all over the place, bits in your hair, in your dinner, in your bed,' she says. 'And the noise! While the darned thing was on you couldn't hear a thing and it took for simply *ages*.' She went on to say that rice farming needed water and sheep required big paddocks. She widowed herself from one and moved to the other, she explains. If you get married you go where your man goes. 'A great part of living, but I preach,' she says, 'is adjusting advantageously to change.'

During the night the ship, as if with her tremendous and hidden heart pounding, after pausing, resumes authority and pursues her mysterious course.

'You had better go,' my widow says gently. But I do not want to leave. We are in her cabin. Closed in and safe. My widow has explained that my tears earlier were travel shock, that when the ship is at anchor in the middle of nowhere it is usual, on a first voyage, to feel as I felt.

'I want to stay,' I tell her. 'Please let me stay in here with you.'

When later I go along to Mr George's cabin I remember the warm sweet bread and milk which was my first meal, mine and Helena's, in the Georges' kitchen. I remember the soft sounds of their voices, the two perplexed people, as they talked to and fro. And then Miss George, warming some milk in a small saucepan, broke some bread into the two little white basins. She poured the milk over the bread and let the basins stand for a few moments. I was nervous that Helena, unaccustomed to the strange mixture, would be rude to the old lady and refuse to eat it. But Helena spooned it up quickly and I did the same.

That night I simply arrived on their doorstep, late, after their locking-up time, exhausted and hungry, having used all my money for the railway journey only to find they were, as they said, *suited*. The advertisement I was answering was in an ancient magazine, apparently. It had not occurred to me to notice the date.

The Georges had found a maid already. They were *suited*.

There was hot water enough, they told me then. If we would like a bath the water was hot and there was a bed which we could share.

Why should I remember the sweet warm bread and milk now? It is almost ten years since that night. I have been with the Georges ten years.

Mr George opens to my small knock. 'Mentor!' he says, 'and susceptible.' He holds out his arms.

'Your father don't ever use the Moseley Road now. He don't ever pass the farm now.' My mother is adopting more and more Mrs Pugh's way of speaking. My mother forgets that she has given this information before. She forgets that she writes it in every letter. 'He comes by Mount Pleasant and the Lane,' she writes. 'It's a bit longer this way and he's late home.'

As I read, my eyes fill with tears so that her careful handwriting is blurred on the page. The pages of her letter are lined and fixed together at the top where they have come off the cheap pad all together.

My widow, never telling anyone where she is, does not receive letters at any of the ports.

'What's the matter now?' my widow, on the long chair beside me, sits up. 'Oh, it's nothing,' I tell her, 'it's nothing.' It's the names of the streets, the familiar names, but how can I tell her anything so silly. The familiar names bring everything back to me with an unexpected rush. I even long for the sound of my mother's voice, some of which springs straight from her letter. The familiar street names, two of them quite unlike the suggestion they carry, Mount Pleasant and the Lane, go alongside empty warehouses and yards and waste ground where the chain shops had been at one time. And the Moseley Road is the road which goes by the hawthorn and the elderberry, by the little meadow and the derelict farm. The sudden memory of the farm buildings, the small kitchen and the even smaller bedroom and the ever present mud, all round the place, make me feel that if I could just step ashore, just now, I could walk there.

It is likely that my father and mother will avoid that road forever.

'Smocks.' I try to tell my widow something, knowing that whenever I cry she will always find out the real reason for my tears. I tell her that both of them, Noël and Felicity, used to wear smocks over their Oxfords.

'Oxfords?' my widow pauses, with her lips pursed for the lipstick she is trying to find in her handbag.

'Yes, dark-grey flannels.'

'Flannels?'

Trousers, I explain to her, worn at Oxford, a special cloth, a special woven cloth, dark and of a very good quality. I tell my widow that Felicity and Noël, in spite of having large hands, were very nimble; 'their smocking was beautiful especially when done in green silk on unbleached calico.' I remind my widow about Noël's illness and how it raced ahead. I remind her that my own illness followed. And I cry a bit more.

While my widow touches up her lips and puts her eyes on

I finish my mother's letter. My mother writes that the photographs I sent from Naples have arrived and that she has shown them to Mrs Pugh.

It looks like a nice young man, very good looking, she's got for herself on that ship, my mother writes what Mrs Pugh has said. They have been trying, my mother goes on, to guess his age and what he does for a living. She wants to know too what Mr George thinks.

The photograph is of my widow who was dressed for the Captain's Table fancy-dress ball at the start of the voyage. For this event she is, because of experience, completely prepared and is wearing a sombrero, thigh boots, a flattering jacket and a shoulder belt packed with cartridges. She tries, at the time, to persuade me to dress up too but I tell her that Mr George does not like parties.

'If you ask me,' the widow says, 'that man wants to eat his cake and keep it.' She turns away saying, over her shoulder, that she'll be keeping company with the pack of widows on board and I am not to worry.

This is not the first time that I have noticed the way in which words seem to fall lightly, with scarcely any enunciation, from her lips. It is almost as if she is not saying them. This time, because she has actually turned away, I want to run after her saying I'm sorry, sorry.

It is a way of speaking which I have come to dread since it seems that, through my clumsiness, the widow is offended. I would never intentionally offend my widow. Often she seems to adopt this speech which, when I think about it, is essentially without syllables, when Mr George is present, and it is then, when I hear her almost swallowing or breathing in her words, that I am uneasy. The uneasiness seems to be Mr George's fault at first, and then it occurs to me that it might be something uncomfortable in the widow herself which causes her to perhaps feel inferior in some way, so that she drops words instead of saying them, often bringing her voice up at the end of sentences as though a question is being asked rather than a fact stated.

121

She could even be doing this on purpose knowing that this slack-mouthed speech can be dismissive, keeping a companion or an acquaintance at a distance. In particular, it does seem as if she alters herself in the presence of Mr George. The other uneasy thing is that my widow does not like to accept even a small thing like an apple saved from the dining table. A refusal in the lightly spoken phrases can be very painful for me because I seem to have very little, in the material sense, to offer.

We go ashore in Bombay, the widow saying it is the last land we can step on before the long passage across the Indian Ocean to Australia. Some white women with shrill English school-girl voices are offering little tours in their own cars to raise money for a charity. These 'guides' come flocking on to the ship.

My widow buys me a lace table cloth from an Indian woman at the side of the road. To one side there are some gaunt dead trees, their branches decorated with vultures perching while others circle slowly, high above the towers where people place their dead relatives and friends. A ritual of funeral which seems unthinkable; the English memsahib explains that it is, at the same time, natural and sensible. 'If you think of the climate,' she says.

'There's a thought,' my widow squeezes my arm. She is pleased, as she puts it, that we are not hampered by my gentleman, and, she says, did I notice how lovely the lacemaker was, such beautiful gentle eyes and how clean and fresh she was in the middle of all the roadside dust. My widow seems to get on with the English memsahib very well. I anticipate, with a sort of pleasure, her moments of mockery which are sure to follow.

'The very next time you feel like howling your head off for nothing,' my widow goes on to remind me to remember the Dhobi laundry and what it would be like to have to work there day in and day out. 'But I preach,' she says. 'Scooze I! And,' she adds, '*Hello! All those ladies trying to sound like the Queen!*'

In the evenings I sometimes wander about the ship reflecting on and comparing my own life with the lives of the other travellers. There is the fat woman who dies. I am quite unable to imagine her life even with the gossip that she was, once upon a time, the most striking Madam in the red-light district of Poona. She has to be wrapped and sewn up in a hessian bag for a midnight funeral. She slides in a secret launching along the silver path the moon makes on a sea, so silent and smooth the surface seems solid as if beaten from precious metals. The Union Jack which, with her last words it is said, she insisted upon, stays afloat, rippling, long after the unwieldy parcel sinks.

The way in which the shipboard corpse is handled reminds me of the log lift ambulance men use when passage for a stretcher is not possible. The widow and I have some small amusement in seeing the Union Jack salvaged by a hand, invisible from the upper deck, casting hook, line and sinker with an enviable accuracy.

I think of the Anglo-Indian teacher on his way to a country school in New South Wales. He is looking forward to it with pleasure. He will be provided with a house there. His whole family are with him. They are all, in the language of my widow, tinted folk, and are immediately blamed for bringing smallpox and other infections on to the ship. The little Indian teacher, father of several thin careworn children and creased with anxiety, rushes about the ship. He is frightened for his sick child, overpowered by his mother-in-law and ignored by his passive and pregnant wife, who repeatedly changes her saris as if nothing concerns her. An ominous sign is that the special games deck for childen is closed. He is at once accused by the nervous passengers. I imagine them, the whole family, banished to their cabin, an overcrowded, miserable hell in the middle of this wide sea and beneath the dome of the blue sky, both suggesting a freedom which is unattainable from a ship – except in the gaze of longing.

The story about the trio being flown out to join the ship

changes from the Schubert trio in E flat major, piano, violin and cello to the Saint Saëns septet, opus 65, for trumpet, piano, double bass and a string quartet, two violins and viola and cello.

'Rumour abounds aboard ship, scooze the clichay,' my widow says.

Several Indian Ocean weddings are announced. And the woman in the toque is robbed for the third time. She is heard declaring everywhere that she has now lost everything. But everything. The last of her furs, her jewels and all the gifts she was taking home, including two enormous dolls from Naples.

'If she ever had them in the first place.' My widow has her own opinions on shipboard robberies as well as on the Captain's weddings.

'Just take a look, willya,' she says. 'Just look at them, Darby and Joan. Imagine! Their choppers both sides of the bed.'

I am in the Tavern Bar with my widow. We are perched on the high stools showing off our suntanned legs. I think of the weddings and wish that I could have one of them.

'Have you ever noticed,' my widow says, breaking the small silence, 'the salty taste on the wineglasses?' She goes on to say that it is a known fact about bars that traces of urine are often detected on wine glasses.

No one notices our legs.

'Why don't you read or spend some time in contemplation of the sea?' Mr George says, when we meet at the rail. We are high up at the stern watching the furrows of white foam which express the inexorable forward journeying of the ship. Seeing the fresh clean sea sliced in this way makes the speed of the ship seem greater.

How can I, Mr George wants to know, without irritation in his voice, waste the voyage, the experience of the voyage, by being so much of the time with this extraordinarily vulgar and nondescript person. 'How can you, Vera, descend to whole conversations about, for example, the cuts of meat? How can you be manipulated, Vera, by someone whose interests are purely superficial and acquisitive?'

'Don't, I want to tell him, please don't.' How can I tell him that I am lonely, that I want to be with him completely, that I am missing my children and am on the edge of tears the whole time except when my widow makes me laugh or makes me feel special by choosing me. How can I speak to Mr George about my widow's tender words in the privacy of her cabin. I want to tell Mr George that I am seeing myself, reflections of my own life, which I do not want to see, in the lives of the other passengers. I want to ask him how will the woman in the toque face her family and her friends without the presents which are so important to them. And what about the little teacher man who is more Indian than Anglo. What waits for him and his uprooted family?

'Do you think,' I ask Mr George, 'that the little school house in the country will have drains? And will there be a water tap?'

Mr George is puzzled by my questions, so I keep to myself the thoughts of the scorn which might be the next thing the Indian teacher might have to face. And I do not mention the successful and popular Madam from Poona and her questionable reception in her deep sea bed.

I tell Mr George that I am stupid, silly really. I tell him that I am missing him dreadfully. And he says that that is *really silly* because he is there on the ship. He teases me a bit about the widow and says he is not able to compete. He does not see me often, he says.

'Perhaps I am too possessive,' he says. We rest against the rail, he has his arm round me and he explains that he finds that he refuses to accept an unchosen friendship and that I must try and understand that. He has a present for me, he says; he has it in his luggage for me, but will give it to me straight away even though it is meant for later.

The book Mr George gives me is by a man called Peter Green and is a biography of Kenneth Grahame. I read of *the herb of self heal of which he had always a shred or two in his pocket* and I resolve to emulate Kenneth Grahame. As I read it, it seems to me that Miss George must know this herb, perhaps under another name. And, if I go further back, Gertrude too. Miss George in particular with all that concerns her, me, for example, my children and her own brother, caring for him all through his life as she has done. All through the years too, she has maintained a serenity in her household so that it becomes for me, during my years of studying, a haven, a place of retreat and sanctuary, where my children are well and happy, their cheeks rosy with the warmth of well being, good fires and food and fresh air. A place where household matters are smooth and efficient. A late realisation, perhaps, in the middle of a long journey, in the middle of my life.

I think of my father, at the beginning of this long journey when I visit them, my mother and my father, before setting out. I forget all too easily about the herb of self heal.

The picture of my father seeing me off is still vivid. He is forever running alongside the train and, when he comes to the end of the platform, he has to stop running and there he stands, his face white and anxious and one arm still raised in a farewell of tender optimism, getting smaller and smaller as the south-bound train pulls away, rounding the great curve away from the railway station.

It is true to say, I tell my widow later, that in the presence of Miss George and her smooth household there is an atmosphere of discretion and peacefulness. This peace seems to me to depend on the Georges together and the children. For a great part of the time I explain I have been away from that household but always looking towards it.

126

An Uncompromising Landfall And The Beehive

I did go back there, I tell my widow; I go back to the farm very early the next morning while it is still dark. I am worried about my bicycle, I tell her, and I want to fetch it. I describe the mist to my widow and tell her that it makes the whole place seem different as though I have come back to the wrong place. The pit mound disappears in a wreath of mist and is transformed in the first light of the dawn as the slag shines with moisture. At first I think it is coal miraculously surfacing and, from the habit of thrift, feel as if I should have a coal search on the mound before doing anything else. Of course I know really that coal can't come to the surface by itself and that there is not much coal to be found in a slag heap. But the paths of light coming up across the sky seem quite magical and it is as if some sort of vision might appear in that desolate place. There is no one there and the place seems strange as if it had been left for a long time. In the half-light things suddenly show up for what they are, a heap of dug potatoes and the broccoli, beaded with tiny water drops, ready to be cut. The kitchen door is open as I left it. The fire is out, but the hearth and the potatoes I put to roast are still warm. I wrap up the potatoes in a bit of newspaper and stuff them in my raincoat pocket. Why waste them, I think then.

I am nervous that Felicity might come, or someone else might come. I go on telling my widow, my mouth stuffed with fried onions, I suddenly have the idea that Felicity might have come back, that she is in the bed upstairs. She might not be nice any longer. There is a sinister side to Felicity and I am afraid. I find two sacks and put potatoes and broccoli in one. And in the other I squash in as much of the hand-woven cloth as I can. I have to tear up a sheet to wrap up the cloth to keep it clean. And, this is the awful part, I have to hack and cut at the cloth to get it off the loom. I feel terrible about Noël's loom. I have to walk with the bike because of the two sacks.

When I reach my mother's house I am sweating terribly and shaking and I realise I must be ill and I feel afraid to go with the doctor's note to the chest X-ray place. I feel certain then that I must have an infection, a patch on my lung. My mother says why am I being so stupid and childish, it's because I haven't had any breakfast. This, from her after all her warnings, and then the breakfast she makes, does make me feel better. So a bit later I go to the farm again, even though my mother says not to. This time I gather as much as I can lay hands on and stuff into the two sacks; books, some of them mine, and kitchen things, cups and cutlery, mostly paid for by me in any case. All the time I am there, I feel that one or both of *them* will return and I have the strange overwhelming belief that it is life and death which is making me do this thing. This kind of robbery.

'It's not in character,' my mother says, when she sees me coming up her path. 'You're like a gypsy,' she says. 'Didn't anyone on the road say something and you with that old kettle tied to the handlebar.'

We give Mrs Pugh some of the potatoes. She never touches cauliflower, she says, and especially not the purple-headed sort. From the woven cloth Mrs Pugh cuts out and tacks in that day three waistcoats, especially tailored for ladies. That evening she tries them on for a fitting with one of her grand customers and sells them with the promise of special silk linings, olive green, gold and cherry, which she has by her, as she says, for a price which, when she tells us, takes our breath away.

'A course,' Mrs Pugh says, 'we'll have a share, the each of us, and there's no need at all to tell any of this to your Dadda. It's a woman's business, this is, which a man don't have any understanding about at all.'

'You moll you!' My shipboard widow is delighted with the story. 'You Moll Flanders!' she says.

It is almost straight after the waistcoats, I tell my widow, that I go for the chest X-ray and Mrs Pugh sews the things for me and the card comes for my admission to the TB farm as she calls it. I did not have to wait at all for the bed.

'A course,' Mrs Pugh says, 'that's on account of you being one of *them*. They look after their own kind,' she says. 'They look after their own kind, they do; if it was me or your mam we'd be waiting till Christmas.'

'You'd think,' my widow says, on hearing Mrs Pugh's reported opinion, 'that it's well worth it to study all those years to get a hospital bed!'

The widow heaves herself over to brown her back. 'To think of you,' she says, 'sitting here on the deck hiding quietly every morning behind the *British Medical Journal* with all that stored up inside you like that. When I think,' she continues, 'when I think of you, from what you tell me, you don't seem to be a person capable of understanding even the advertisements in a women's fashion magazine let alone a medical journal.' She sighs. 'So naïve you seem to be.' The widow pronounces it nave. This is something she does on purpose like calling Burgundy B'jundy and Proust the way it is spelled.

'All this that you've been telling me,' my widow says, 'it's better than the book of the film.' This sets her off growling and laughing and then she coughs her way over to the ship's rail and flings her little cigar overboard.

'I'm giving 'em up. No worries!' she says. And then she is suddenly serious, wanting to know what I am.

'What exactly are you?' she says. Am I the sweet English sixth-form girl, she wants to know, or am I a very clever intelligent woman hiding behind a clear youthful complexion and a remarkable and convincing innocence.

When I tell my widow the difference in our ages, Mr George's and mine, is something like twenty-two years, she is quite calm about it saying that in her book, it's better to be a sugar daddy's plaything than a slave for a princeling and his progeny. We are both amazed at her astute observation and what she calls her superb use of the vernacular, every bit as good as Shakespeare, that we go off at once to the bar to perch once more on the high stools to see if anyone will be captivated, as she says, by our legs. My widow, in particular, has very shapely legs.

'Haven't you ever noticed your own?' she asks me, when I mention hers. It is while we are there in the Tavern Bar, very close now to our destination, that my widow in a low voice warns me about gold diggers who might flatter an ageing man and get his fortune away from him and, at the same time, deprive me.

'Ageing men are terrible fools,' she says. 'They can be made fools of so easily.' She says that we must watch out for parading pick ups among our fellow passengers. I point out that Mr George does not have a fortune.

'He has a very handsome face and demeanour,' the widow says. 'He's very nice looking, distinguished *and* he's an *intellectual* . . .' She breaks off to say that the ship's shop has a charming display of enamel. A special sort of enamelling with patterns outlined in different colours. 'It's called *cloissoné*,' she says, 'it's something we must see and, if we like it enough, must have.'

The widow tells me later that she is, as she says, unable to make me out; she tells me that I am quietly dignified at times and, at other times I howl like a baby. I tell her that I suppose she is right.

130

There are times, she tells me, when we have to be dignified, or try to be, because of circumstances and the circumstances themselves often preclude dignity. As we so often are, we are both amazed at this spontaneous shrewd wisdom, so well expressed. 'I like to think,' my widow preens herself, 'that during our long voyage, I have initiated you, helped you in some way.'

I have to tell my widow that my destination, I explain I don't like this word, that the place I am about to reach, frightens me. I tell her that I am not at all dignified and controlled as she suggests, and, holding in my hand the little enamelled brooch which she has just given me, I begin to cry.

'Listen!' the widow says, 'hold your noise, as your Mrs Pugh would say. When I said just now that you had a nice complexion and intelligence I failed to say that your hair is awful, it's terrible, it's pathetic, everything that can be wrong with hair is on your head. Listen!' she says, 'why don't the two of us duck in now and get us a hair do.'

Later, when we are standing in a long line, with all the passengers, on the deck, waiting for the routine fingernail and forearm examination by medical officers from Customs before disembarking, my widow, jerking her head towards the wharf and the sheds, tells me that the first people to arrive at this place took one look at the nondescript uninviting landscape and started swearing. 'And,' she says, 'they went on swearing and we've been swearing ever since.'

My widow, I notice, is starting to inhale and swallow her words. 'They went on swearing and we've been swearing ever since,' she repeats what she has just said in that particular way she has, of not enunciating the consonant with the vowel, as she does when she is not quite at ease. She usually goes from this way of speaking to what I call her fruitcake voice. I wait for it trying to think if I have upset her in some way.

131

'It's called a Beehive,' I tell Mr George, as we stand together, at the ship's rail after the medical examination and he is able to leave the queue and come across to where I am waiting. I pat my puffed-up pile of hair.

'They call it a Beehive,' I tell him. 'That's what my hair is called. Beehive.'

'I expect the style suits your friend,' Mr George says. His left hand trembles as he places it alongside my right hand on the rail. We look across together at the uncompromising landfall.

SHIP AND WHEELCHAIR

It is at times like this, when in some sort of suspended state, perhaps on board ship, or walking steadily behind the smooth purring of a wheelchair, there is the half-remembered idea of having my father's two hands next to mine on the throbbing rail of the ship. There is the possibility too that, as the rail of the ship rises slowly above the horizon and just as slowly sinks below the horizon, he may be the next person to walk towards me on the deck giving the impression that he has walked on the waters of all the oceans in order, as has always been his custom with buses and trains, to see me off or to meet me on arrival.

It is during moments of glancing memory like this, that it seems easily possible to step a little to one side and be able to walk from the end of the road, where we lived and on to the worn narrow field path which made a short cut to the main road and the row of little shops there, grocer, greengrocer, post office and chemist. The field path seems now to have made a link between childhood and the responsibility which comes afterwards. I began, in this responsibility, to carry home fourteen pounds of potatoes, seven pounds in each of two bags.

Then there were the conspiratorial closings of the bedroom door during discussions between my mother and my father's sister, my aunt, about the Christmas dolls, the picture books, the new dresses and the prospect of being taken out to tea in a tea shop where there was a lady violinist, whose name my mother knew, and a gentleman who accompanied the lady and her violin on the piano.

And then there was the time when this sister came and cried and cried for a whole afternoon and my mother with her limited English then, tried to comfort her. I wished so much that day that my father would come home early and *dismount* from his bicycle and whistle for us to come out to meet him at the gate. But he was, that day, taking his boys from school down the coal mine. He was always taking his boys round a factory, down the mine or to the Municipal swimming baths.

'Does he have doubts about paternity, your gentleman?' the rice-farm widow, my new friend on the ship, asks me more than once. 'Does he admit paternity?'

'It's something we don't talk about,' I begin to tell her. And then Mr George comes. The next person to come towards me on the deck is *not* my father stepping lightly across the washed boards after walking on the waves to see us off through Suez.

'Rumour has it,' the widow says, 'that this will be the last ship to go through Suez. Imagine,' she says, 'all the apples in subsequent ships going rotten. Imagine, this journey through Panama and round the Cape!'

Before following the two of them, my widow and Mr George, down the brass-bound stairs to the dining room, I pause to allow myself to catch once more a tiny glimpse in my mind of the place where the field path comes out on the main road. At this place there is a house where a hairdresser lives. She cuts people's hair in her own front room, and while you are sitting there, in a sheet, with your hair pinned up in a topknot, you can see the people emerging from the field path and waiting to cross the main road. The bus stop is at this place too, immediately outside the hairdresser's house.

My aunt, when she comes on the bus to visit, cloched in beige velour with a grosgrain trim and her nervous fox fur, its little legs dangling, slipping to one side on her narrow shoulders, climbs down from the bus and comes towards me telling me, straight away, that I am growing too fast, that my dress is too short and too tight and asking me how did I come to crack, already, one of the lenses in my spectacles.

All this belongs to another time and is pushed back there when I reach my widow at the table, and she reminds me again, while Mr George is reading the menu, that the world is a place of couples.

'The whole world,' she says, 'is for couples.'

THE PLAGAL CADENCE

Your father must have been coming home by the Moseley Road. Your father has been run over and killed by a lorry in the Moseley Road. They say he died at once, but a policeman said he died in the ambulance. Your father, my mother writes, must have been coming home by the Moseley Road. She writes that she had to go to identify him. He is lying, she writes, on a bed, a sort of stretcher when they take me in to see him. He is all covered up except for a small part of his face. He does not look as I know him to look. I have never seen an injured or dead person before. They tell me he has a lot of injuries all over his body. The place on the Moseley Road is spread over with sand but his blood shows through. Mrs Pugh is asking why your father was coming by the Moseley Road since he don't use ever that road. I am telling Mrs Pugh I don't know why he was coming home by the Moseley Road instead of Mount Pleasant and the Lane. I know Mount Pleasant and the Lane is longer, but he would not have been in a hurry. There is no hurry for either of us and Mrs Pugh says there is no hurry for her either. We shan't ever know, Mrs Pugh says, why he was coming home on the Moseley Road.

Mr George is listening for the plagal cadence in the Gregorian chants when I arrive at his apartment. He has this nice university flat near the campus; I live at the hospital.

He pulls off the headphones and takes me in his arms and I feel his heart beating in his warm chest. I cry about my father's death. The letter has taken about a week to reach me, I tell Mr George, so I have to understand that all this time my father has been dead and he says that is so and that my father will be buried already. The voices, without ebullient pride, sustain their harmony in the headphones lying on the table. I imagine the singers in clothes made of rough cloth, standing, their feet cold on a stone floor and, for a moment, the apparent detachment from our lives and way of living seems desirable and comforting.

Die mit Tränen säen, werden mit Freuden ernten. 'They that sow in tears shall reap in joy,' my mother translates for me. Her letter is, as usual, a mixture. Herself over-laid by Mrs Pugh. She writes that though she knows my father will not be coming home, she watches the clock expecting him, 'any minute now'.

My father's life-long belief, that the life we have is simply a forerunner for something else (he called it 'everlasting life'), rescues me. I imagine him gathered up safely off the Moseley Road, safe and comfortable for ever and peaceful. I think I can even know the place by the elderberry bushes where the road curves. I can see the road clearly in my mind and this place is where he will have been lifted up. When I tell Mr George this he says the Moseley Road might be quite different, quite changed now.

We have to go out for groceries. We have three nights together, a whole long weekend, after what seems to have been an endless separation, a fortnight during which we have both been under the strain of our new work. As Mr George says, our time together is very precious.

My beehive is a mess. I try brushing. My head itches dreadfully. Brushing makes it worse. I simply do not know what to do with my awful hair.

These apartments, I tell Mr George, are so noisy, you could have records and not bother with headphones. The headphones cut out the noise from other people he explains. And then he tells me, all in a rush, that he has been looking forward to this weekend tremendously and that he does not want us to live apart. I understand that I have been, selfishly, as usual, simply thinking about my own difficulties in a new appointment. I almost always think about my own sense of being alone and I forget about his.

Mr George says that he thinks we should look for an apartment where we can live together. He says too that he will need to accept and give invitations and that he wants me to be a part of this new life. I say that I think I shall be good at this and that I can quickly become a hostess and inherit a dinner service from a department store. I am making the mistake, I tell him, of trying to see the whole of our lives in one long weekend, trying to cram in a whole future at once so that I can't breathe. He says we must live a little bit at a time.

In the greengrocer's, overcome by the fragrance of the peaches, the plums and the nectarines, I buy a heap of fruit and another of vegetables. Mr George is studying the grocery part of the shop. He is out of place in front of these crammed shelves. He is not his usual neat self, his pullover is wrinkled and he has deep creases in his face which is red from too much sun. His shoulders sag and, twice, on the way back to the apartment, he pauses to have a rest.

'Perhaps I should learn to wear less,' he apologises, 'it's the heat. I am the only person wearing a woollen pullover.'

Catching sight of myself reflected in a shop window, I tell him that I'm not much of a dish myself, in fact I'm more bedraggled than he is, and that when we have taken the shopping home he is to have a rest while I go out to find a hairdresser.

My summer frock, my English summer frock from several previous summers, is rumpled, washed out and ugly. My sandals are shabby too. I look a mess, I tell Mr George; in the bright sunlight everything we have looks old and worn out. In the face of Mr George's fatigue and my mother's letter it seems selfish to be considering things like hair and clothes. My widow is miles away. I wish for her, for her energy and her advice and, in particular, her way of regarding things, and the way she could laugh.

I never talk about my widow to Mr George. I had to understand, on the ship, that he did not like her. It was strange to have to learn this when I have known him for a long time and when I have always presumed that I, being loved by him, know all there is to know about him.

Mr George has a shower and I leave him to rest while I go out again. It is a surprise when Mr George, as I am leaving, says that he thinks I will be missing my new friend and that shopping will not be as pleasurable without her.

'Precisely this gift you have,' he says, 'of being able to have friends, which are not perhaps of the supreme or ultimate choice, is a gift which you must always use because it is a help to you and, in turn, can be of use to other people too.' He adds that he does not have this gift. He even regrets this.

It is like having a Blessing from Mr George and I feel cheerful when I go out in to the afternoon which is still full of sunlight and blue sky. There is something about the clear brightness which makes me feel shy and conspicuous. The shops have a flimsy temporary appearance and I have no idea which one to avoid and which one to enter. Twice I nearly walk into a verandah post. There is no one alongside to give my arm a pinch and to say, 'You must have this,' and 'For heaven's sake don't, *do not* buy that colour.'

Ahead of me on the pavement is a young woman with two children, clinging one on either side of her. I remember seeing them as passengers on the ship. I pretend not to see them, they reflect my own shyness and lack of confidence. I recognise, unwillingly, myself in them. They walk, all three, close together, uncertain and tired, looking without seeing at the unfamiliar shops.

I feel suddenly afraid that I shall not find either a hairdresser or a dress shop.

When I think of the ship's shop and the daily overwhelming

display crowding the smallness, I am amazed to realise how someone must have ordered and packed the incredible quantity of merchandise especially chosen to satisfy the needs of passengers in their boredom. I wish that I had allowed the widow to buy me a dress when she wanted to. I could have chosen anything then. She wanted to give me one more present, she said then, and I refused it. The cut of a dress or a jacket, she told me, matters so much. She said that in choosing a dress it was necessary to know the kind of seams and the exact positioning of the seams. 'Seams in the right places and little slashings offering glimpses of the body, not usually seen; like the underneath part of the breast can be very sexy,' she said then. And she described the fold and the fall of the material against the hips and the thighs and, especially, good fitting was essential on the shoulders.

'Honestly,' my widow said, 'your wardrobe's a mess. You don't seem to care one bit about fashion. You have a way of looking, not poor exactly, but as if you are unconcerned about money. You look as if someone throwing out their old clothes has let them fall on you. And then, at the same time, you are elegant. You do have a natural elegance but you simply don't know how to make the most of it.'

My widow is right. I have not the slightest idea how to make the most of myself, especially with clothes. I think of her presents, the shorts, the little black handbag scattered with sequins, the scarves, which she promised would be tender, and the *cloisonné* brooch and suddenly it is as if she is telling me to go straight in to the next dress shop with the idea of choosing something with a low neck and without sleeves, either in white or with the clean colours of the *cloisonné*, and to forget how terribly English and shabby I am.

I can't think why your father did not die in his sleep, my mother writes. *It would have been so much better for him*. I carry her letter squashed in my pocket. I always felt my father would live for ever. That is the impression he gave. I suppose he had this feeling about himself and has passed on the idea, because I too think that I shall go on living – and not as an old helpless woman, but with the same strength and energy I have now.

For years it seems I have talked to and listened to my father in my head. I have always thought of him as being there at home whenever I should go back there. I remember that when he saw me off on the train, when I was leaving for the ship, he reminded me that he was getting older. He said that on no account was I to rush back to Britain in the event of either my mother or him being ill. He seemed then to have far more sense of the enormous distance which I only found out about as, slowly, that distance was covered. He said too that people who made this particular journey, at a certain time in their lives, often did not return but stayed in the new place. He gave, for an example, Mrs Pugh's two brothers. It is only now that I seem able to take this in.

It seems, in my life, that my father has shown me everything, especially things like being able to feel the quality of the air, and to see what he described as lovely scenery or a fine view.

I understand now, I tell Mr George, that I never thanked my father for the gifts of looking and feeling.

'I think,' Mr George says, 'that he would not have expected you to.'

Mr George runs his hands over my clean short hair. He says he likes it cut this way, that it suits me. He says he likes my new dress. It is the first white dress I have ever had.

'Broderie anglaise,' I tell him, 'that is what these small embroidered holes are called.'

Mr George says that the dress, in a charming way, resembles a petticoat. And in the evening he helps me to take it off.

'Your father didn't know he was going to die today.' I re-read my mother's letter. 'Not knowing,' she writes, 'he left a piece from his breakfast against coming home hungry.'

For years, I can think now and remember, for years I have seen my father carefully put aside something from one meal to save it for his next.

If I have for all this time talked to my father in my head, asking his advice and telling him things, there is no reason why I should not go on asking him and telling him. After all, it has always seemed to me that when I pray *Our Father* it is *My Father* I see.

During the previous week Mr George has, as a surprise for me, bought a record player. He has borrowed from the music department in the university the records of *Fidelio*. Mr George has this quality, which I lack, of knowing something and not telling it until the most suitable time.

I do not mention the dinner service, but during the music I think about it. I think about saucepans and cutlery and a set of wine glasses. I am excited and I want to talk about these things to Mr George and to ask him about the people, *the couples*, the people described by my widow. Because of not talking about this I am not able to stop talking about Florestan's cry from the dungeon and the part, in the story, where the prisoners, having been given the freedom of the daylight and sweetness of fresh air, emerge.

'I know,' I tell Mr George, 'that people say that Beethoven wrote for human voices as if they were musical instruments and that, because of this, the opera is ungraceful, but I don't agree, not at all!'

I manage, in the magic of the music and the little enclosed world of our weekend together, to make a mint sauce. My haircut makes me feel neat and quick. I wash the mint and chop it finely and put it with some sugar and vinegar in a cup all in the time it takes for the *Fidelio* overture on a seventy-eight.

Another nice thing about our weekend is that Mr George suggests that we go for a walk in the evening after dinner. He says that in this way we can put off going to bed and have a longer time to look forward to the night.

'Let me help you out of your Edwardian underwear,' Mr George says, when we return. It is our second night together out of the three, and once again, he helps me to take off the new dress.

WHEELCHAIR ... ROADS

Once more I explain to Mr George that Miss Eleanor has not gone out and that she is not expected home any minute. I explain that she simply is not here any more.

'Shall we think of something else?' I say. 'Can you try to remember something else?' I ask him.

I am wishing for Miss Eleanor too. After all this time I wish for her. I wish for the sight of her approaching, tall, angular, energetic, her complexion clear and her light blue eyes always intelligent and always kind. I think of her hair brushed and scraped back and fastened in a bun on the back of her neck, the only style she allowed herself. It suited her.

At eighty-one she wondered why she was so healthy and again at ninety-one and even at ninety-seven . . .

I am wishing for the sound of Miss Eleanor's voice as Mr George wishes for it.

One of the happiest moments in my life which I have never forgotten is because of Miss Eleanor. It was when she offered me thirty shillings a week and keep for Helena and me. This included two hot baths a week for both Helena and me and days off in a row so that I could make the journey to the Midlands to visit my mother.

Wheelchair in Hammond Road. Wheelchair rumbling over rough blue-chip surface. The moon rising quickly is a half moon, perhaps a little less.

'Can you try to remember something or someone else?' I try again, my heels clattering as I rush the wheelchair rough rough on the blue-chip metal.

'Are those your heels, Vera?' Mr George wants to know. 'Vera, are those your heels?'

'Yes,' I tell him. 'Yes.'

'Horsey Horsey don't you stop,' Mr George seems to be singing, 'just let your feet go clippetty clop.' Was that song, he wants to know, before the war or during the war or after the war? I tell him I have no idea. I had forgotten the song, a silly song, and it is something strange about memory, Mr George's memory, that a song like this one should come into his head just now.

The storm clouds have parted enough to allow the red and purple sunset to deepen the colour of the winter trees. The flame trees in particular are vivid, the red flowers bunched in between the yellow berries of the crowding cape lilacs. The blue chip is speckled with bruised and bird-pecked berries and the cape lilac branches are starved on the winter sky. The dusk comes quickly. There is not much light from a moon on the wane.

Mr George tells me, when I ask him, that he has no idea at all what he had for lunch and this worries him until I remind him that it is Friday and we had fish and chips.

'Yes, it was a nice piece of fish.' Conventional good manners come to his rescue. He remembers in his well-bred way, knowing that he should remember.

At the corner of Hammond and Goldsworthy we wait in the pale-moon silence to cross the quiet road. We notice, as always, that the noisy birds, the parrots, the magpies and the doves are quiet at last. Mr George tries to remember a line from the poem 'Margaret'.

'Wordsworth,' he says, '*to my heart convey* . . . What comes next, Vera, what comes next?' And I tell him; '*so still an image of tranquillity*.' And he says that is the line he wants.

We cross Goldsworthy and go on down Bernard. I remember the poem is one of the poems marked by Mr George, in pencil, with Miss Eleanor's name. The book was always beside his bed. Once, when we are tidying up, Miss Eleanor and I, Miss Eleanor says to leave the book on the chair where it is. 'He likes to linger in its glance,' she says then.

Yesterday, Rachel writes, *I attended a natural childbirth. It was in the woman's own house, a home birth, as she requested. I ended up sitting with the husband on the floor, each of us in a fisherman's oil skin. A beautiful baby, a boy nine and a half pounds* . . .

While I am thinking of the letter and wondering whether to explain to Mr George about Rachel being submerged in the waters of childbed, Mr George begins to tell me that, this morning, he means to go over to the British Museum but is a little late getting out of the house . . . Meanwhile, overhead, there is some stirring among the settled birds as if a fresh argument is being raised, even if half heartedly, over some roosting differences.

Shall I explain to Mr George that it is now the evening and not the morning and that he is not going to any museum? Shall I, instead, talk to him about Rachel? This Rachel. This pink tiny nymph of a daughter, this Rachel delivering an enormous child for an unknown woman. A woman unknown to us. This Rachel, the tiny neat little girl reared in pink and white embroidery and learning to speak with Miss Eleanor's clipped and precise accents. This little girl who, it seemed, grew behind my back, to become tall like Mr George and Miss George.

For some reason just now I remember showing Mr George a photograph of Rachel sitting dishevelled and sweet in her pram. I tell him I like the photograph very much. He likes the photograph too and holds it with reverence smiling at it. As I watch him looking at the photograph I see that I have to realise that his eyes and his smile are not directed at the child but rather on his own sweet briar hedge, which is a full flowering background surrounding the pram. He is completely absorbed in his own impenetrable hedge . . .

When I actually see the direction of his gaze and knowing, as I do know, that Rachel is Mr George's daughter, *as only I can really know*, the sudden understanding is like the flash of awareness which accompanies learning something new from a textbook or even a literary work or a fiction. A rite of passage, a celebration of learning as if, in this moment, I have studied a long book. It is a sudden vision of the kind after which a person can never be quite the same again.

One morning I open the door into the fragrant steam of the bathroom and there is this child rising tall from her bath to reach for the towel. There she is, all at once it seems, grown up, tall, long-limbed and graceful, rounded and smooth and a delicate shell pink, her skin glowing with youth and the hot bath, and she quite unaware of her own fresh loveliness. She seems then untouched and untroubled. When I think about this now I understand that I was never like this, or if I was once, perhaps briefly, on the edge of this innocence and smooth youthfulness, the time came and went by without my noticing any of it, without my noticing my own body and how I might look as a young woman. I have no idea . . .

'I have no idea,' I say to the back of Mr George's neck. 'I have no idea,' I say, 'what I was like, years ago. I mean, a long time ago.' The wheelchair runs smooth smooth now on Bernard Street. Really guided only by my fingertips. I hardly need to make any effort.

Mr George wants to know what it was I said, so I tell him once more about not having any idea of what I looked like when I was young. Mr George's rug is slipping, so I stop and tuck it round his high-pointed knees. He seems to ponder my remark.

'Look!' Mr George says. 'There are the fresh new leaves coming on the plane trees.' And when I look up and along the deserted street I can just see, in the half light, the green leaves bursting out along the branches. The whole street is miraculously arched with a delicate green leafiness. The whole length of the street. It is just like Mr George to be the one, the one out of the two of us, to notice first that the plane trees are coming into leaf.

As I walk, smooth smooth, with the wheelchair I think I will try to stop living in the way I am living. I am forever trying to get through what I am doing, to get one thing after another finished and *out of the way* only to find, of course, that there is nothing in particular waiting for me.

I must try to remember to think about Mr George seeing the leaves.

Sometimes I would, at her invitation, look through some of Miss George's treasures. A photograph of Mr George as a boy dressed in a heavy tweed suit and with a certain puffiness about the eyes. Miss George particularly is proud of the expensive good quality tweed. I search the childish face for the man. I read eagerly, then, to find very little about Mr George on his old school reports carefully kept by Miss George without, I suspect, his knowing. Hardly anything is on the reports, his height and his chest measurements from one term to the next and English Literature seeming to be the only subject reported on. When I remarked on this to Miss George she would give her little laugh and say that her brother never cared for any mathematics or science.

A newspaper photograph survives of a queue of people in London in the early 1930s. Mr George is pictured quite clearly as a young man, a member of the Fabian Society, Miss George explains. They were protesting against something called the means test, she says. It was during the Great Depression, she adds, feeling sure it was because of the means test and to do with education cuts.

I would like to talk to Mr George as I used to. I always asked him everything and I told him all that was on my mind.

I want, just now, to ask him if he remembers being pleased with the Pullman when he used to travel to visit me. The luxurious Pullman with the rich paintwork and polished panelling and the white embroidered antimacassars and the firm upholstery and the pictures of castles and their battlements from all over the British Isles.

Did he look forward to visiting me, I want to ask him. But I do not ask him because he might not remember. In the same way I do not ask him if he remembers the sudden fresh green leaves of the plane trees in London and how he once wrote to tell me he was pleased to have found some accommodation within walking distance of the British Museum.

'What do you remember?' I ask him one more time as we turn into the next street. 'What do you remember, Mr George?'

'The fear of conception, Vera, the fear of conception,' Mr George replies.

Waiting Room
(The First)

These days I live with the need to have something lined up to do next. The way in which I live reminds me of a joke; there are two goldfish swimming round and round in a goldfish bowl and one fish is telling the other fish that there's no time to chat as it's one of those 'get things done' days.

I make little lists because I might forget what I am doing, or more importantly, what I am going to do. Like going to the doctor's to see if my moles are cancer, like throwing away leftover food, old clothes, letters and other papers, especially receipts and bank statements saved over a great many years in case of a possible taxation audit (random).

It's when I am sitting in waiting rooms that I take stock of the way things are, of the way I'm living and of the way I used to live. I compare my life with other people's lives in a rather superficial way. Not comparisons about money but rather on the quality of roof beams, joists, floor boards and the sizes and shapes of windows.

I go back in my thoughts quite often. One time I actually try to remember all the names of the hospitals in the city where I lived for years in the English Midlands. There was, at that time, the Hospital for the Diseases of Women, the Sick

Children's, the Ear, Nose and Throat, the Skin Hospital, the Fever, the Cancer, the General, the Accident (Queens) and the Queen Elizabeth. The QE was Maternity as well. I manage to stop the litany before going on to the names of streets, churches, schools and shops, though the names of houses come to mind – Sans Souci, Barclay, The Hollies, Padua, St Cloud and Prenton. Naturally the hedges follow, the closely watched hedges, the laurel and the privet, the rhododendrons and the holly, evergreens in a series of repetitive quartets.

Those hedges from another country have given way to the honeysuckle, the hibiscus, the oleander, the plumbago, the white and pink climbing roses, the wistaria and the geraniums. There are too the street lawns, the box trees, the plane trees, the peppermints and the cape lilacs. But perhaps it is the blue metal, the smooth and the rough, which I notice the most when we are walking. The habit of closely watching the hedges is not lost, if anything it is more intense, and intensely too, the roads. The roads are closely watched; Harold Hammond Goldsworthy Bernard the park Thompson Koeppe Princess Caxton Warwick and Queen and back Queen Warwick Caxton . . .

I need a shrink, I say to myself, and go on to say that shrink is not a word I use. The use of it, even if not said aloud, is an indication that I need someone with specialist training.

Really this place! All I seem able to do here is to stare at the other people. We all seem stupid sitting here with a conventional obedience which is expected of us.

The chairs here are all joined together, fixed, making a square space in the middle where children can play. There are some little chairs and a low table for the children. I forget about myself for a bit, when I see a small child staggering about with a big plastic bucket. He has thick dark curls and a pale face and I pity him throwing up so much that he has to take a bucket around.

What's the matter with me, I think then, because 'throwing up' is a phrase I never use; neither do I say 'around' instead of round. I dismiss all this immediately when I see that the child

152

is loading up the bucket with all the toys, the building blocks and farm animals, provided for *all* the children to play with, and is hauling them off to the safe harbour between his squatting mother's possessive spread-out legs.

A man sitting diagonally opposite gives his urine specimen to his wife to hold and she takes it and goes on reading her magazine holding the thing as if she was a specimen-glass holder, as if it is meant that she should just sit there, holding this specimen glass while he sits back stroking his chin and raising his eyebrows in every direction in turn round the waiting room; *see here everybody, meet the wife, my specimen-glass holder.*

The receptionist behind the curved desk has a commanding view of the whole room. When I look at her it is clear to me that she would prefer a dress shop in a not too classy department store. A place in which she could peek round the fitting-room curtains saying with emphasis, 'it's *you* dear' either for a dress, a blouse or a hat. It is probable that the pay is better in the Outpatients' Clinic and the hours less barbaric, especially since the decision not to have the clinic open at all on Fridays. I notice every time, without really meaning to, that she wears mostly red dresses or blouses with low V-neck lines exposing the healthy unworried skin of a woman approaching middle age and a suggestion of a similarly healthy and unworried bosom, more or less out of sight.

Certain days are set aside for walking sticks, crutches and wheelchairs. On these days I remind myself often to count my blessings and to remember that there are people worse off etc. For one thing I am only accompanying a patient and am not a patient myself. Without meaning to, against my will, I notice that some of the patients have a perpetually grieved look and some seem actually to be parading their disability. They exaggerate a grieved way of walking with one shoulder higher than the other, the body turned inwards on itself and the head tilted to one side. They seem to have the special skill of taking up the whole width of any place and then there's no way of getting round them like when you're waiting to go down in the small elevator to the Lab for blood tests. Sometimes people, like these people and unfortunate, will take up all the room in the aisles in the supermarket. Walking on two sticks, lurching first to one side and then the other, they make it impossible for anyone else to pass or even reach round for a tin of dog food, a cereal or some soap powder.

I suppose all this sounds cruel and without sympathy. It is not meant to. I might be on two sticks myself one day. Such thoughts, like everything else at present, are very out of character. Like this morning when there are no oranges to squeeze I am shaken to discover how much the disappearance of a small ritual can disturb me and cause an inability to go on to the next thing – just because one insignificant part of the morning routine is missing.

When I ask Mr George what he had for lunch he does not remember and when I ask was it nice, what he had for lunch, he says that it was very nice and, because it was nice, it is a pity that he does not remember what it was.

It is a pity, he says, to forget something nice.

An occupational therapist, with knitting needles pushed into her hair which is dressed in a firm grey bun, approaches. She has cut, she tells me, some pieces, squares and circles, of foam cushion material. She gives them to me saying that she knows relatives and friends enjoy being involved. She says that making little chintzy covers for these is a nice way of spending the long afternoons. She calls her pieces soft splints for pressure areas. She smiles with real pleasure.

I want to tell her that I don't have long afternoons except in my consulting rooms and I am not able to sew there. I nearly explain that I can't sew, it's a bit like not being able to dance, I mean ballroom dancing, it is always an embarrassment to say, 'I can't dance.' It is the same with sewing.

I can imagine all too easily the sense of futility which would all too quickly obliterate the hopefulness accompanying the giving of these chintz covers to some of my afternoon appointments who do, indeed, need occupation and direction but who have, at the same time, the ability in the face of offered activity to make the activity seem useless and unnecessary. This attribute is of course a symptom of the cause which might not be cured by the covering of soft splints with fragments of a cheerful material.

I take the pieces all the same and squash them into my brief case.

THE SECOND WAITING ROOM

Then there is the wheelchair. I have to attend to the wheelchair.

In Wheelchair City all the years of clinics, of examination rooms, of X-ray departments, of physiotherapy cubicles and the desks in reception halls pile up as if I am going from one to another and to the next and the next. The wheelchair-engineering-department waiting room is, in reality, nothing more than the corridor lined with various orthopaedic appliances and devices and, of course, wheelchairs to suit every need.

I ask the secretary, when she telephones with the appointment, if I could come and fetch the new foam cushion myself. No, she says, the patient and the wheelchair have not been seen for over six months. Both must be brought in for the appointment.

It is during the time of waiting that I imagine my widow standing alone in a well-watered plot, a green place in the middle of the wheat paddocks. Her house sprawls behind her, a cool well-painted place, held by seams of green like an extravagant embroidery on a background of varying light and shade as the clouds move across. I remember my widow telling me she took short cuts. She made sandwiches, I suppose, instead of cooking dinner. I remember her ordering for me at table on the ship. She had ideas. One time the two of us have a fruit platter, all

157

different kinds of fruit cut up and arranged in a design. Fresh pineapple rings, mango, paw paw, banana, peeled and sliced peaches, strawberries and a scattering of frozen raspberries and blueberries lightly sugared. With this we have a white, crisp bread roll, some fresh butter and a glass of white wine each, very cold.

I can make a fruit platter instead of the dinner. For some time I have been buying too much food. I have been preparing too much food unwittingly and throwing it away. A roasted leg of lamb, a whole chicken, a large handful of Vienna sausages, two lots of topside mince – actually made into dishes with macaroni (one) and rice (the other) – and countless carrots, onions, potatoes, green and red peppers, mushrooms and zucchini. You name it – I've thrown it away.

Courgette, it occurs to me just now, is a pretty name for a certain type of housemaid or a little dog or for a prostitute with an unblemished record. It is because of thinking of my widow that I have these ideas about courgette being a pretty name.

'Have you ever noticed,' my widow asks me one day on the ship when we are in our usual haunt by the swimming pool, 'that women when they are naked are unable to resist looking at each other's legs.'

I tell her that we are not naked.

'As good as,' she says. And she tells me to come to her cabin. On the way she jerks her head towards the Lounge Bar where there is a little knot of passengers.

'The war's been over, how long?' my widow says. 'The war's been over twenty years,' she says, 'and that woman's still telling how she was bombed out, how she lost everything in the bombing in London, in Hackney, South-East.'

I tell my widow that I have noticed her and that every day she finds a different listener for her unforgettable dreadful experience.

'You should never ever,' the widow replies, 'stick on one thing like that. All she's doing is feeding the bad time and making it last for ever.'

Remembering this now I think it is the kind of thing Gertrude would have said. I remember too how easily we, by the end of the war, accepted heaps of rubble. All this mess which accompanied our living, broken bricks and glass and slates everywhere and often, at the end of a shabby mean street, a bomb crater or a boarded-up shop. The people when the war was over, linked arms in great long lines in the streets and danced 'The Lambeth Walk' and 'Knees up Mother Brown' and 'Run Rabbit Run'. The women with curlers in their hair and the men in shirt sleeves did not seem to notice that some houses had whole fronts and sides missing. Some were tarpaulined and boarded up but others showed pink and blue wallpaper, torn and discoloured. These houses looked like dolls' houses, opened, but without the magic. It is easy now, in the wheelchair waiting room, to recall all this, especially my loneliness then which seemed to be reflected by a small thin black cat, ugly because it was poor and alone, trying to vomit at the edge of the ruined buildings alongside the dancing people. I was alone and pregnant and sick. I remember now that, when I tell my widow about this dancing after the war, she reminds me that at the *outbreak* some people, *bloodthirsty*, danced in the streets. She reminds me that she was in London herself then and, in an attempt to go home to Australia, was held up in Cairo. When she tells me about Cairo she explains all over again how body hair was regarded as something undesirable and a special body-hair-remover woman, in a sort of yashmak, turned up once a week to attend to all the ladies in the house.

'Can you imagine!' I almost hear my widow's growling laugh which invariably becomes a cough. 'She used some sort of honey paste. Honey and almond. Marzipan!'

'Couldn't we be married now on the ship?' I ask Mr George one evening when we are leaning on the rail on the top deck.

'Like those other people,' I say. 'The Captain is marrying couples.' I tell him, 'There are weddings almost every day . . .'

I can see at once the whole idea is distasteful to Mr George, the idea of being conspicuous in this way and being a part, as he says then, of something cheap, a vulgar superficial celebration instead of something private and tender. Shipboard life, he says then, is not natural. It is an enclosed world in which everything is somewhat heightened and exaggerated. A ship is not a place for the making of decisions except, of course, those made in the course of duty, by the Captain.

As I watch Mr George being lifted up now by two competent men in biscuit-coloured work coats I understand something about myself and that is that housekeeping and shopping have become something of an act of the will.

The biscuit-coloured men make some alteration to the new cushion. They lift Mr George a second time and the therapist replaces the old cushion with the new one.

It is exactly how Mr George is that he is the one to notice two magnolia flowers, the colour and the texture, he thinks, of fresh cream, high up in the rough-leaved tree. I tell him I am not able, any longer, to climb into the branches of a tree. Does he remember, I ask him, that I did, once upon a time, climb up for a flower which, from below, looked perfect.

He says he is sorry he does not remember and will I remind him.

That's it, I tell him, I simply climbed up for a flower. I do not tell him that I discovered then that the great flower, which was pure and white from below, was sunburned brown and withered and beginning to go rotten.

THE THIRD WAITING ROOM

Now I am acquainted with another kind of waiting room. This is a silent place and I am the only person waiting.

There are two young receptionists behind a high grey and silver counter. They are both young and pretty. They have well-developed telephone voices. They, on appearance, seem disdainful and apparently without thoughts but having the power, unspoken, not even known about, to cause a client disturbance and a careworn feeling beforehand about what to wear for the appointment. As I said, they do not know they have this power. It is not their fault.

The walls are grey, decorated with a pink pattern. The carpet is thick and grey. The elevator glides without noise behind automatic doors, which are the same grey as the walls making it difficult to see which is the way out. Some paintings in gouache and gold leaf hang in strategic places. The imitation marble tubs sprout growths of realistic fleshy leaves. On the whole it is a restful place. Secretly I touch the leaves, knowing them to be artificial.

I understand perfectly why I am waiting here. Ordinarily I would never sit in a place like this. And, ordinarily, I would never be in the position of seeing the fine beads of perspiration on a stranger's upper lip as he studies the papers on the table in front of him when we are alone together in his office. He is particularly careful not to make mistakes.

In this reception hall there are no surgical appliances, no lists on the walls about the importance of vegetables, about menopause support groups, the need for bicycle helmets and the dangers of smoking. There is nothing about this place to give any evidence of the particular problems and the kind of consultations dealt with in this building except the revealing little outbreaks of moisture on the forehead and the upper lip which accompany concentration during consultation.

I am too early for my appointment having misjudged the distance, the traffic flow and the number of intersections with traffic lights moving, one lot after the other, through four changes.

I am sorry to have to be the one to tell you . . .

I take out Mrs Pugh's letter to read it again.

I am sorry to have to be the one to tell you, as how your Mam passed away very peaceful early this a.m. Your mam she came to the gate to tell me she felt cold. I feel cold your Mam tells me and I tell her now you go straight back to your bed and I'll fetch you over a nice cup of tea, nice and hot. Well I fill the hot water bottle and I go down to the corner to the phone box to ask the Dr. to come but by the time he come She is gone and he did come straight in about 1/4 of an hour he was at the door. Shes gone I tell him straight away. You will be glad to know she went that quick and from what I know no pain. I must tell you that you writing your wedding to her give her your Mam great happiness. There is 1/2 a letter she'd wrote you I will put in the post as you will be glad to have her Blessing. She does not know a Miss Gladys Moore she tells me when she 1st has your letter. This Miss Moore her who came in off the road to be Witness at the Registry or the other name. She does not know it either.

I know she would hope them to be Good Friends to You.
Your Mam is the best Friend to me all the years. I want you
to know we been Good Friends. I don't have Her to talk to
now . . .

It is several years since I received the letter from Mrs Pugh.
I keep it with other letters in my handbag and, at times, when
I am too early in a waiting room, I take it out and read it again
and feel comforted that my mother is safely dead and buried.
She had to live some time longer than my father. While he was
alive, she told him everything. She had to manage without him
for some years.

I do not know Miss Gladys Moore and I do not remember
the other person's name, a man. Both very kindly made
themselves late for work that morning by stepping, at my
request, into the Registry Office at ten-past-eight. Mr George
and I were first off on the list to be married that day. This Miss
Moore, she enjoyed it the most. She said she loved weddings.
She was the happiest one there and her eyes shone. And she kissed
me.

When I am here in this cool quietness it is clear to me that
there are a great many people who would never need to wait
here. They would never experience the discreet harmony of
armchairs, low glass-topped tables and untouched magazines.
At intervals with tiny sighings, the receptionists lift the receivers
from the muted telephones. The receptionists' faces are empty
of emotion, enough emptiness to enable them to spend whole
days, weeks, months, even years in this place. The softness of
their youthful complexions and of the pink and cream of their
clothes merges with the general soothing quality of the room
which cushions the hardness of the enormous building and its
many floors devoted to human well being. The individual is
often not able, beyond a certain point, to look after, completely,
his own body and his own possessions. Consultations about
health and about possessions require complete trust between
client and consultant.

I understand perfectly that it is because of money that I am waiting here.

MY WIDOW'S HOUSE

It seems to me when I think about it and I do think often, like now in this waiting room, that I never saw the homestead again as I saw it that first afternoon when the sun, already low immediately above a blurred and distant horizon, sent long shadows from the trees at the near end of the paddock.

When we arrive that afternoon, my widow and I, the house is nestled in green, in a well-watered plot, she says, like she imagines the place in *Electra* where Orestes fulfils his destiny and slices his mother's lover in half during a barbecue.

The place is green to the windows and the door. Green hedges, green painted gates and green, dark-green sad pines close together, a green embroidery stitched with firm green seams into a corner of the pale bleached land.

The house is really two houses held together with paint and the verandahs, which are the best part of the house. She is forever painting the place. Start at one end, she tells me, paint right through and start again. She oils the floor boards and keeps some rooms clean and aired for guests.

She has what looks like a little village of houses for the men and their families and there are sheds for itinerant workers. She shows me as much as she can before it is dark. The silence is incredible. I tell her I love the smell of her land. And when darkness falls it is a black impenetrable darkness and it comes quickly with a cold wind as in the desert.

Like my mother's house, my widow's house stands open to the

164

spring, to all the seasons, the doors propped open with ancient flat irons and the cast-iron ornamental claws, which were once bath feet. My widow pauses on the threshold to satisfy herself that the scattered droppings are from possums and not from rats.

All night the pines sigh outside the open window. The next day we change the shelf paper in the kitchen and the storeroom.

'Print,' the widow tells me, 'especially the pages of the specials in the newspaper, keeps the cockroaches away. Epsom salts are good,' she says, and scatters the shelves with the clean white crystals. 'Imagine!' she says, 'the cockroaches after their dose.'

Golden Fleece

'Loquats,' my widow says, 'you never tried them? Try one now. They are like lamb's-wool, gold tipped, caught in the deep branches of the tree when they are ripe.'

My widow has had, as I have, too much to drink. She surpasses herself, she says, in poetic imagery. She never thought I would come, she says, and she is unable to hide her delight. 'You have come! Dear child!' she says.

'Come out into the paddock,' she says. The kiss the widow gives me at the edge of the paddock is not a pale, cool-lipped brushing of a powdered cheek crumpling against mine.

THE DORIAN SWORD

It is a well-made Dorian sword. My widow stands with the rifle. 'Throw off your buckled cloak,' she says, 'and grasp it firm.' She then comes gently up behind me, slowly putting the rifle in position, telling me in the most loving and persuasive tones to look a little at the beauty of it and to handle this beauty. And, raising it for me, she tells me to look along the well-cared-for barrel. She tells me to shoot.

'Of course you can,' my widow says, 'and of course you want to. It is just the same here as it was on the ship, isn't it?'

WEIGHT

'I've always been about nine stone ten,' my widow says during the tenderness of a rest on the unbuckled cloak. We watch, together, the thin smoke drift from her dark little cigar. I breathe in this smoke. I breathe in her refreshment. '*I do love you, Widow*,' I say.

'I thought,' she says, 'that you would not come. I thought, after all this time, it would be too difficult for you to get away.'

I explain that I am having a short holiday, that I have finished my appointed term at the hospital and have set up in private practice. I tell her I intend to stay in Australia and I explain that Mr George has gone to Scotland for a visit and will be coming back. 'I daresay we shall have a lot of travelling to do because of the girls and Miss George,' I say.

'Well, air travel and all that, easy even if expensive,' the widow says. 'And Migrant, even if we don't never see each other again, *I don't dislike you*! How's that for a double negative?'

166

Together we contemplate the peaceful blue sky.

'But about my weight,' she says, 'I put it on and then lose it and revert to my birth weight, nine stone ten or eleven, give or take a pound.' She confesses to having broken a toilet once in Italy. 'A very cheap place it was, you understand, Migrant.'

Her third husband paid for it.

Later I am still contemplating the wide dome of the blue sky and my widow is studying minutely the quality of the earth.

A First Husband

'I was married,' my widow tells me, the day she is trying to teach me how to sit a horse. 'I was married straight out of boarding school and we went straight to Europe for my *finishing*. The parents, both sides, insisted. The custom, you see, with the well-to-do. One property making a marriage with another. You knew from Christmas parties, from about the age of six and on to teenage tennis weekends, more or less, whose wife you'd be and which house would be yours. It was a bit like being in the cattle sheds at the Royal Show.

'Terrible eating habits in boarding school,' she says, 'packets of biscuits between meals, whole packets, that sort of thing. Fat with spotty faces, but mostly fat.'

My widow explains that a first husband should always be acknowledged like a first publication of something, even if it's not particularly good. She has been married three times and has made several pastoral changes and additions. If she thinks of her husbands at all, she thinks mainly of her first one. She has always maintained that it is necessary, in life, to be capable of change and to move along with changes. She has herself gone from rice to beef and then to sheep and wheat and sometimes wheat and beef, give or take the poultry. She has owned and lived in different places. We leave the horse.

THE THIRD HUSBAND

'For my third wedding,' my widow tells me, 'I had a grey dress, rat grey. I did not see the colour properly until I was actually through the ceremony. Grey, colour of rat, I said to myself, and stuffed it behind the wardrobe in the hotel room.

She tells me that her third husband wore a four-button virgin alpaca jacket, $1995.00, a cable-stitch hand-knitted cashmere cardigan, $1925.00, narrow velvet corduroy trousers, a steal at $395.00, and ostrich gloves at $700.00. The gloves might have been emu. Not counting his underwear, his shirt, his hat, his socks and shoes (genuine python), and the gold in his teeth, he stood at $5015.00. It was pounds actually, she explains, but she has put it into dollars, roughly, to give an idea of the value now.

'For entertainment at the Breakfast,' my widow says, 'we had a woman performer who used her dress as a musical instrument. With weddings,' she goes on, 'it is best to stick to convention. White, vanilla or parchment, for the first, *café au lait* for the second and grey for the third, pearl grey not rat. I errored there, Migrant, just as you are going to error with that black. If you insist on black you should add something pink. This cheap little pink scarf, perfectly hideous on its own, will do something for your black. You need a little tender glow with black.'

'I can't make up my mind,' my widow says in the evening. 'Simply can't choose between outfits, the Gertrude Stein or the Shirley Temple.' She stands dishevelled and disconsolate with clothes all over the bedroom.

THE KISS

'Oh! For *Heaven's Sake*, Migrant! What's all the fuss, it's only the two of us for dinner. A coupla snags on the barbie out there. Kiss me! Migrant,' my widow says. 'Oo's got a kiss for Aunty?'

We have both been quenching our thirst, foolishly, with beer.

MORNINGS

The light here, in the early morning, is as if washed. A small cooling wind causes the net of green branches and leaves immediately outside the window to sway and tremble. In this light even the untidy bedroom scattered with discarded clothes has its own order. The light comes dust freckled and leaf shadowed on the unwashed window. It makes a tremulous pattern which moves gradually down the wallpaper on the opposite wall as the sun rises higher in the morning sky. We do not hurry to get up some mornings.

Other mornings we are off to some distant place, some corner of fencing the widow wants to inspect. No one in the world (including Mr George) knows where we are. And always when we return, the homestead looks different.

SOUNDS WHICH REMIND

On my last morning at my widow's house there is a grinding noise from outside, a persistent groaning and straining as of trees being uprooted. It is a reminder for me of the tanks passing through the village, where my school was, during mobilisation at the outbreak of the war. And then I think of Mr George and the straining and creaking of the branches of an old tree outside his window and how he does not want the tree cut down. He says the noise reminds him of the creaking of the timbers of a great ship.

One thought leading to another; my mother is a widow for some years before she dies and is strictly eligible to be on my little list of widows. In thinking like this I am paying homage to her. Perhaps here I should acknowledge the enormous changes she was capable of, I mean how differently she conducted herself in speech and mannerisms when reading *Faust* with Mr Berrington, compared with later on when her widow, Mrs Pugh next door, was practically her sole companion.

Being capable of change, as my widow says, is tremendously important even if some things never change in spite of surrounding changes. An example being my mother never changing the way in which she walked. She placed her elegant feet, toes pointing down, one before the other, never stumbling or making an awkward ugly movement. Always, in my mind, I see my mother's well-bred feet fitted precisely at the heels, her ankles poised in good quality shoes, well made and not needing to follow the dictates of fashion. Similarly, my mother, reared first on Caruso and then on Tauber, would say that the contemporary tenor sounded as if he had been eating too much red meat but she would, in spite of this opinion, be able to listen with pleasure to the qualities in the voice of a new singer.

My widow tells me the noise is because the tractors are moving off to make the miles of firebreak. I am amazed at my widow and her apparent carefree nonchalance, and I ask her if she is not at all overcome by so much land and at having to manage the men and the seasons.

'Migrant,' my widow says, 'I don't manage the men and the seasons. They manage me.'

RAMSDEN

'You don't mean to tell me,' my widow says, 'Migrant, you do not mean to tell me that this woman, a mature woman, a staff nurse or charge nurse, as you call her, actually wore ankle socks over her stockings. Bobby-soxers!'

We are having a couple for the road, my widow's words, before leaving for the long drive to the airport.

I tell my widow that it might have been in my imagination only. I tell her that, though certain music recalls Ramsden vividly, the cello concerto of Boccarini and some cello of Vivaldi, I never actually heard this music with Ramsden. And, as for the neat ankle socks when she is walking in a storm of rain beneath massive beech trees, I do see her clearly wearing these socks under the dripping trees, but it's only imagined. I never walked anywhere with Ramsden, only perhaps several respectful yards behind her along a hospital corridor, and even then she would be walking with another staff nurse, the two of them rustling along in conversation with *each other*. I tell my widow, 'I tried to explain to Ramsden, at least I *wanted to tell* staff nurse Ramsden about the downward thrust of the cello and about the perfection in the way the other instruments come up to meet the cello, but I never did tell her.'

'So you told your gentleman about it, instead.' My widow's

171

tone changes and she is breathing in her words hardly enunciating them. 'I bet you did! Just as soon as you could!'

'You are the only person,' I say quickly, 'to whom I have said that I had this thought – that someone had carefully measured the movements of the notes controlling the going down and the coming up in order to produce this exquisite mixture.' As I am telling her this I am not sure if I am being truthful or not. But this ceases to matter when she says, in her ordinary voice once more, that it is a known fact that women are *better together* at measuring and controlling. I am grateful for the emphasis.

In the car I explain that, during the war, we all did wear ankle socks over our stockings. The habit was both an economy and a way of keeping warm.

STILL THE THIRD WAITING ROOM

I am still sitting here waiting in this grey and pink reception place, the third waiting room. It surprises me that I am alone here, the widow, my widow, being naturally close in my thoughts. It is because of my widow that I am here.

I did not walk anywhere with Ramsden and when I see her that time, sitting near me in the suburban train (except for her white hair she looks the same and is within reaching distance), I intend to speak to her and, with that strange feeling that there will be another time for my intention, I let that chance go. Similarly, I intend to visit my widow. Once more, I let a chance go . . .

I do not go again to visit her after the first time. There is always something to prevent me from taking that particular direction, which is more complicated than simply crossing the enormous continent. It is as though I have been moving on and away, wrapped up in what I have to do and absorbed in what concerns my work and me. Perhaps it is simply that I let the intention and chance go – yet again. Perhaps this is what I am like.

My widow writes to me one last time. A letter I still have every intention of answering though I understand I have let that chance pass too.

In this last letter she is about to leave for distant places on the other side of the world. She means to concentrate on France and Spain because of her recent lessons in French and Spanish. '*Japanese next and then I'll go to Japan . . . Ginza here I come, but first Paris and Madrid*!' Her exuberance touches me because I have not replied to earlier letters.

> *All my life, Migrant, I've been able to change with the changes but this time I'm beat. If a tree is uprooted or the wires down . . . If a tree falls, I'm scared. And I've got no one to scream to if I almost step on a snake. You might wonder why I travel so often,*

the widow writes. She had always thought, she writes, that without the obligations and the constant work of looking after someone, that she would really be free to enjoy the farm, that she would be free to go off all day if she wanted to. Free for a shoot or a swim and without having to get back home quickly but, as it turns out, all this freedom is hollow and lonely and the place has become alien, an alien place.

> *I am alienated from the place by the place. I'm nervous here. I hardly ever sit down let alone lie back watching the clouds as I do on board a ship or even peering from a plane. I guess, Migrant, that's why I travel. You will come, Migrant?*
>
> *You will come again, Migrant, won't you, soon?*

173

I pause in my re-reading of the crumpled letter which lies with others at the bottom of my handbag. It seems that the property is a place to worry about. A fallen tree is frightening and not simply a source of firewood. She dreams of disasters, of thieves, of land supposed to be hers but not resembling her land. She dreams that sinister people are camping in places where she might unexpectedly come upon them. She pictures herself swimming and trapped alone, at dusk, by a root hidden under water. She imagines a woman sitting in the hollow of the land, with her geese, on a filthy nest hatching goslings. She thinks of this as the nearest approach to happiness a human being can hope for, to be at one with life, she writes. She writes that she thinks she is going mad.

The accountant tells me to travel. He says the money is working very well for me. And he says it is up to me to make the money do what Mrs Ruperts would have wanted for me. *He* suggests *travel*.

The uttering of her name in his calm and rather pleasant voice gives me, as it always does, a shock. During that time I was with her we always called each other Widow and Migrant, using these names frequently in third-person narrative as though we were both impartial and devoid of an excess of emotion. And then, often, we each enclosed the other in some special word or phrase of endearment.

Her death was special and in character in that she, my widow, was the only one killed in an accident when the bus, filled with tourists, went off the edge of a road in the Pyrénees. I imagine her, with a crowd of widows, singing on the bus, buying souvenirs, speaking lately learned French with extra gestures and stammerings intended to sound as French as possible and, most likely, making for herself a special Friend in the crowd, not necessarily a widow but someone with certain qualities of need.

It is years since I have seen my widow. She will have died enjoying herself. I nearly say this aloud to the accountant to

174

take his mind off my shabby unfashionable clothes. He wants me to know that I have enough money and am able to spend some, he is trying, tactfully, to tell me this, on clothes.

When I think of money I think of it in terms of the way I was brought up. It is as if I shall hear forever the voice of Mrs Pugh, my mother's widow, saying, 'more money than sense' and 'tek care of the pence and the pounds 'ull tek care of theirselves' and 'a fool and her money is soon parted,' like the refrain in an ancient ballad, telling a well-known story, or in a modern popular song, in which comment is made on some human disaster.

Church Bells

I had an aquarium, just a small one, in here for some time. And then, one day, a patient starts screaming. She tries to cover her breasts, her pubic area and her face screaming that the expression in the eyes of, as she says, the most hideous of tropical fish, reminds her of her husband and the way he looks when he is about to climax.

I tell her that I'll get the firm to fetch the aquarium straight away. It is only rented in any case.

This small waiting room, furnished with shabby chintz and tattered magazines, has in one corner a stained machine complete with paper cups and a particularly tasteless instant blend. This waiting room is mine. When I sit down in here for the first time ever, during all these years, I hear the church bells. The bells cannot be heard in my consulting room which is, of course, sound proof. The bell ringers are practising and the repeated and reassuring peal is carried on the wind. It is like hearing the church bells across the fields when I was at school years ago. The whole school, on Sunday mornings, took to the field paths to walk to the Meeting House, which was in the next village, and which had no belfry and no outward call to worship. These bells, recalling those other bells bring back the summer morning mist, the soft voice of the cuckoo calling across the fields of wet grass and the sweet breath of herded cows waiting near a gate. This mist heralds, what we called in England, a fine day.

When I think about the third waiting room I have no way of knowing the hopes and expectations of the receptionists there. I can see for myself, from the results, the care with which they have dressed themselves and attended to their hair, and the ways in which, with cosmetics, they have transformed their young and innocent faces to the artificial, either the demure or the knowing. But there is no way of knowing their expectations or their ultimate realisation of what their lives have to offer. In spite of the confidence inspired by being encapsulated in exquisite pink and grey tones and the impersonal elegance of carefully chosen cream or white blouses, authoritative tailored skirts and high heels, the minute lines of discontent begin to form, unseen, causing the sweet rosy mouths to become thin lipped and slack with the beginnings of a realised unhappiness. A number of such people will experience some kind of waiting room sooner or later. Statistics show this.

My widow always maintained that a woman should never lean forwards over a mirror or a man.

'Lie on your back, Migrant, and hold the mirror up,' she tells me this several times. 'Hold the mirror up and a decade will slip back into your pillow. Lean forward,' she warns, 'and you'll need two porters to carry your bags.' Perhaps I shall be able to pass on this advice at some time.

My own receptionist is fat and untidy. One of her legs is shorter than the other. She has an ugly limp. She has a moustache and an inordinate curiosity about people. My patients confide in her and her appearance consoles the nervous especially those who do not know what to wear for their appointment. She comes breathless, apologetic and late, a swirling mid-calf pandemonium of clashing colours laden with strips of black lace heavy-like braid, her floral armpits wet.

'*Ach! Ich schwitze,*' she says, in her mother tongue, and sits in the waiting room to rest her feet, gossiping as if waiting for a consultation herself. She likes, in her own words, a small dose of *Schadenfreude* and to enjoy the remains of human nature. She used to smoke but managed to give it up when I was obliged to have a 'no smoking' sign on the wall.

Sometimes there is a small excitement, during which her Teutonic love of order and discipline and an unexpected gentleness in her ability to carry out this criterion of behaviour are very useful.

I remember the widow asking me, during my one visit to the homestead, why I continued with my work and why had I changed from surgery to general practice. When I try to explain to her about the helplessness experienced in all forms of medicine, I remember Noël saying something about the ultimate choice I would have to make between being a surgeon, a physician or what he described, with unnecessary unkindness, as a cheap psychiatrist. He, at that time, was cynical with a rapidly advancing illness of his own. He said then that I would be attempting to deal with medical and surgical conditions for which there are no remedies except those surviving from folk tales and legends . . . 'Mythology,' he said then, 'and witchcraft.'

At the time, I try to explain to my widow, that some things manifest themselves openly – an eye for example, dislodged by cancer, lying on the stained gauze when the dressing is removed – yet other things are wrapped up, remaining unseen in hidden wishes, in blame and remorse and in accusation.

When I contemplate my work like this I can see that cause and effect are more easily seen in outward harm, and the secret unseen flight into illness is the one which does not show itself clearly and is knitted to a destiny, from which there is no escape, and which contradicts all cherished ambitions and hopes.

The jewelled and pleated elegance of the doves strutting on the path is not disturbed when tempests of self-doubt, panic and fear approach my door. The glowing colours of the warm bricks are reflected in the serene breasts of the doves. A pleasant image. A remedy.

I have to tell my widow, when she asks me, that I have no explanations. I do not pass on anything from my work but carry it myself in my experience. There is a great deal that has to be known and, at the same time, it must stay hidden in the heart.

To the questions, is there a Balm and is there a Physician? my answer is, yes. There is trust, there is courage and there is kindness. These are the ingredients. And anyone can be the Physician.

I suppose homelessness, the sense of not having a place of sanctuary to return to, can come at any time, even in such separate places as the Great Bitter Lake where a ship might wait for a passage through the Suez Canal, or in the quiet suburban streets where the winter trees are finely drawn on the cold rosiness of the winter sunset.

Perhaps the homelessness comes about because of the lack of immediate links with immediate surroundings. The Great Bitter Lake because of the silence and the strange colourless calm water, and the suburb which shares the same lack of concern. The traveller is the more susceptible to this apparent emptiness and might concentrate on some detail close enough for minute examination, the whitening of the knuckles on the hands clutching the steady rail of the ship, waiting at anchor, or the innocence of the nape of the neck exposed and vulnerable.

In an unfamiliar park, one time, when Mr George, half-remembering, asks me, 'Where shall we eat our sandwiches?' I have no answer suitable. In the unfamiliar park the ugly toilet block seems to be the only building and, beyond that, no consoling view of any kind.

The church bells are repeating and repeating, still, their expected measured and exuberant movement of sound; the next falling sounds ringing out over the first falling sounds. The sustained pealing fills the afternoon and my waiting room. The light is changing.

Our walk is smooth smooth humming and purring along Goldsworthy and smooth smooth down Bernard, westward to the park. Because of the blue-chip metal Hammond is rough. From behind the wheelchair there is a close view of the back of the neck of the person sitting in the chair. The back of the neck, the nape, is vulnerable.

Bay Road, Harold, Hammond and Goldsworthy, Bernard Street, the park, Thompson Road, Koeppe Road, Princess, Caxton, Warwick and Queen. Of these closely watched roads Goldsworthy is smooth and Hammond, because of the blue chip, is rough. Bernard slopes, Queen is fragrant and shaded with the old trees we call the peppermints. Whereas Hammond has cape lilacs and plane trees which arch overhead, the sunlight dappled on the green leaves. These trees meeting overhead, as they do, create either a shelter from the sun when it is too hot, or from the rain when it comes.

There is something about the changing light of the afternoon which reminds Mr George of that time of the day when people start returning to their houses.

'Is Helena in yet?' he asks. And a little later; 'Is Rachel in?' I remind him that Helena and Rachel are both living and working in London and that they are coming to visit at Christmas. He expects, he says, that Miss Eleanor will be home shortly.

I do not remind him any more that Miss Eleanor will not be coming, that we can no longer expect Miss Eleanor to come home. I leave it as if it is still the three of us, Mr George and Miss George, the Georges and me.

Queen Street Warwick Caxton, cross Princess into Koeppe down Thompson to the park, we are on the way back. Thompson like Goldsworthy is smooth smooth . . .

'Is Father in?' Mr George's question surprises me. The thought of a possible father for Mr George takes me completely by surprise, that there was someone, that there was a father I know nothing about and have never thought about. A father, someone he will have known and expected home. Someone he called 'Father'. A whole fresh experience lies in the small question. Miss Eleanor, she too, will have called this man, this stranger, 'Father'. They will have been together. How were they when they were together? Brother and sister and Father.

'What did you say?' I ask Mr George. In his quiet dignified way he tells me he is sorry, he is a silly old man and has forgotten what he said. He is holding a white paper napkin and, with great care, he spreads it out on his rug and then begins to fold it.

I watch the hedges closely as I walk, the honeysuckle, the hibiscus, the oleander, the plumbago, the white and pink climbing roses, the wistaria and the geraniums. There are too the street lawns with the box trees, the plane trees, the peppermints and the cape lilacs.

Perhaps because of Mr George's small question, the surprise in his three words, reminding of another entirely different place, these hedges give way, for the time being, to that series of repetitive quartets, the evergreens, the laurel and the privet, the rhododendrons and the holly.

The hedges, the streets, the gardens, the houses and the people, the couples. We, Mr George and I, are a couple.

'We do not seem to be like a couple.' I say.

'Vera, what is it you are saying? What did you say, Vera?' Mr George wants to know.

'We do not,' I tell him, 'seem to be like a couple.'

'Why do you bother, Vera,' Mr George replies, 'with such an ugly word?'